Ramses'
and
The Labyrinth of The Crocodiles

by

John-Richard Thompson

Sketches and Illustrations by Felicity Jammpot
Maps by Sharrif Aziz
Photographs by Alistair Jammpot, Ph.D.

Copyright © 2024 John-Richard Thompson
All rights reserved.
ISBN: 979-8-218-39961-0

Rascal Press
New York, NY

For
Joan & Edwin Thompson

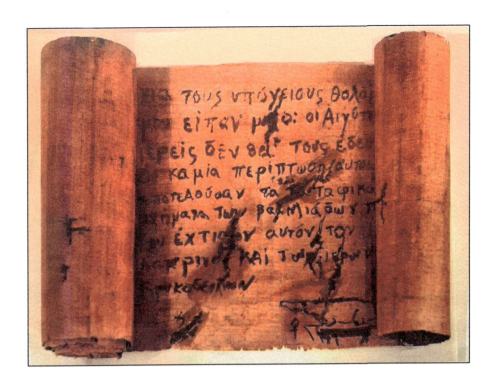

"…of the underground chambers I was only told: the Egyptian priests would by no means show them, these being the burial tombs of the kings who built this Labyrinth, and of the Sacred Crocodiles."

Herodotus[*1] *– Histories, Book II*

Translation:
Lancelot Achilles Simeonidis
Curator, Greek Antiquities
University of Atlantis, 1899

---

[1] Note: words marked with * may be found in a glossary at the back of the book.

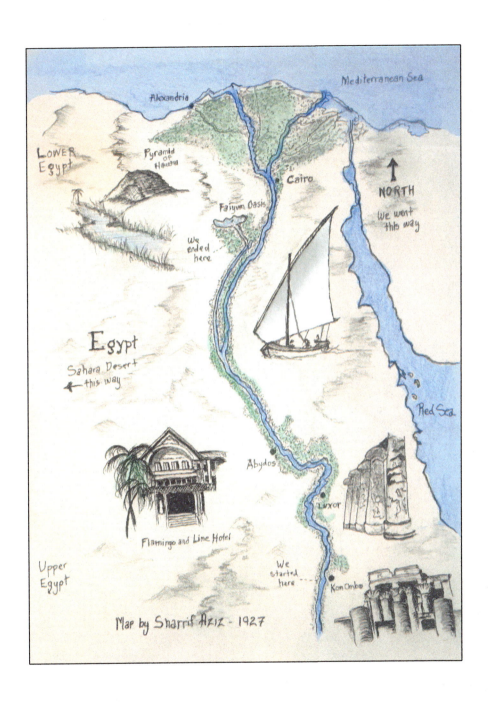

1.

THE TEMPLE OF KOM OMBO

Ramses Faro

1

One starless, moonless night a long time ago – a very, *very* long time ago – a hissing, slithery Egyptian cobra with a black eye patch and a jagged scar upon his snout called through a broken wall. "More light!"

A scrawny, toothless man climbed into the hidden chamber and held up a torch. Firelight glistened on the hieroglyphs*, the symbols and brilliant paintings of the pharaoh and of Sobek*, the crocodile-headed god of the Nile. The cobra's band of tomb robbers had already cleared out all the treasure and he wanted to make one last slither to be sure they had left nothing of value behind.

He oozed over broken splinters of wood and shattered pottery. He squirmed along piles of linens, now grey with age.

Behind one of these, the cobra discovered a small wooden box, about twelve inches long and ten inches high. It looked like a small sarcophagus* with a lid carved to look like a bundle of reeds. He coiled around it and read the hieroglyphs etched into the top:

Wherein Lies the Key to the Labyrinth of the Crocodiles

"Is it posssssible?" he whispered. "Wherein liesss the Key..."

"Key to what?" asked the scrawny, toothless man.

The cobra ignored him. "Labyrinth*...crocodilessss," he hissed to himself.

"Crocodiles!" said the man. The hidden chamber lay within sight of the Nile. What if one of those ferocious beasts had found its way inside?

"Fear not. The Labyrinth of the Crocodilessss liesssss far from here." The cobra tightened his coils, but the sarcophagus would not break. "Open it."

The man used his knife to pry open the lid. It crackled on its leather hinges, and he gasped with surprise. He lifted out a statue of a crocodile made of fired clay colored with a blue glaze. A tiny gold medallion sparkled around its neck. The cobra stared with his greedy eye and flicked his forked tongue at the hieroglyphs etched upon its back. "Take it," he said. "The ssssarcophagusss too."

The scrawny, toothless man reached for the wooden box but froze at the sound of a scream from beyond the broken wall. Cries of terror followed. "Timsah!!" they cried over and over. "*Timsah!*"

"Come!" the cobra snapped. The man followed, carrying the blue crocodile but leaving the sarcophagus behind.

Outside, they discovered their stolen loot scattered before the walls of the great Temple of Kom Ombo*. Not a single thief or robber remained in sight. "Cowardssss!" the cobra snarled. "Sssssslithering away at the first howl of a jackal. Gather this gold before the temple guardssss arrive."

The man did not move.

The cobra looked at him and the scrawny, toothless man's expression startled him – staring, terrified, every trace of color drained from his face.

A shadow crossed over the temple wall.

The man squealed and dropped the torch. He dropped the crocodile statue. He backed up against the wall. His foot kicked a layer of sand over the little blue crocodile.

The cobra spun around, and he froze in place, staring.

If he had warm blood, it would have run cold.

If he had fur, it would have risen straight up.

If he had soft skin, it would have rippled with gooseflesh.

A man, but not a man, stood tall and muscled in the torchlight. He had the powerful chest of a man and the arms and legs of a man. He wore a man's royal white kilt, but he was *not* a man. Instead of a man's head, he had the grey leathery head of a crocodile!

His cold eyes shimmered in the firelight. Evil yellow teeth lined his half-opened jaws.

"Sobek!" the cobra cried, shocked to his core. Three enormous Nile crocodiles emerged from the shadows with their unblinking eyes focused upon the thieves.

"The snake made me do it," whined the scrawny, toothless man as he cowered against the wall. "Take him!"

With a vicious hiss, the cobra struck at his companion. He missed but did not try a second time. He did not have to.

The crocodile-god's three devoted servants surged forward with a roar. Sand flew. Palm leaves scattered. The cobra raced across the courtyard and was already beyond the temple grounds when the screams ended with a crunch, a snap, and a blood-curdling chomp.

2

Years later – many hundreds of years later, Professor Alistair Jammpot held the little crocodile up to the firelight. "Egyptian blue," he said. "It's a glaze called faience*, used for sacred objects to give them the never-ending splendor of the sky." He turned the statue over in his hand. "A magnificent find. Well done, Felicity."

"Thank you, Uncle Alistair," said his twelve-year old niece. She popped a dried date into her mouth and returned to her sketchpad. "Thank Sharrif too," she said. "I would never have seen it if he hadn't tripped over that stone."

Felicity's best friend, the camel-boy Sharrif, sat cross-legged in front of their tent wearing his usual long black robe and dusty sandals. "Accident," he said with a broad smile.

"A lucky one," Uncle Alistair noted. He ran his finger over the blue crocodile. "Hieroglyphs on its belly, larger ones on its back. It will take some time to translate this. In the meantime, I'd prefer you two not go mucking about in that temple."

"But I was hoping we might find something more," Felicity said. "We'll be fine, Uncle. We'll stay with Ramses."

"It is one thing for Ramses Faro to go poking his snout about in places where it doesn't belong, but you?" Uncle Alistair gazed past the campfire at the ruins of Kom Ombo towering above the palms. "There are dangers in there, especially at night. Loose stones. Hidden chambers. Possible reptiles. Speaking of which…" He pointed at the riverbank where several crocodiles lounged upon the shore in the fading sunlight. "I'd prefer you stay away from the river too."

"We'll be careful."

He shook his head. "I've told you time and again, you will be free to explore on your own once you reach your tenth birthday."

"But I'm twelve!" Felicity exclaimed.

Uncle Alistair blinked with amazement and smoothed down his silky black mustache. "Are you really? But that would mean...Sharrif, you're not six?"

"Six!" the boy exclaimed. "I was ten when you and Felicity met me for the first time. I'll be twelve in three months."

"Good heavens, where *does* the time go?" Uncle Alistair muttered, still amazed. "Very well. But do not let Ramses out of your sight." He called past the fire to a bundle of reddish-brown fur curled up in the sand behind Felicity. "You hear that, Ramses?"

A single pointed ear poked up from the bundle. "Quite impossible not to," the bundle said.

"Take a look at this, won't you?"

The bundle uncurled into a sleek Abyssinian cat with ridiculously large ears. He stretched and brushed against Felicity and his golden-green eyes sparkled behind his wire-rimmed spectacles.

"A look at what?" asked the feline Egyptologist, Ramses Faro. He stretched again with his front paws extended far out in front, his chest low to the sand, and his tail curled up like a question mark.

Uncle Alistair held up the miniature reptile. He had cleaned off centuries of grime and its blue faience glaze glistened and the tiny gold medallion around its neck shimmered. "These hieroglyphs on its back..."

"The Sacred Crocodile Sleeps in the Reeds where Lies his Gold," Ramses said from the other side of the fire.

"How could you possibly know that?" asked Uncle Alistair. Ramses blinked over his spectacles. "Oh, that's right, your eyes," Uncle Alistair murmured. "Can spot a sand fly at a thousand paces."

"The Sacred Crocodile Sleeps in the Reeds where Lies his Gold," Felicity repeated. "Which reeds?"

"And what gold?" asked Sharrif.

"It doesn't say," Uncle Alistair returned. "We may find the answer in the writing on its belly."

Sharrif could not read hieroglyphs. He tried to learn but found it all too confusing. He was far more interested in the living crocodiles on the sandbank and a felucca* sailboat upon the Nile with its sail flapping as it approached the nearby village of Ombos.

Uncle Alistair slapped his knees with both hands and rose to his feet. "Right then, off I go. I should like to translate those very same belly hieroglyphs before the museum gets it."

Ramses twitched one of his ridiculously large ears. "Might I ask, Jammpot," (he never called him Alistair and he certainly never called him Uncle Alistair. For him it was Jammpot, always Jammpot). "Why would the museum get it?"

"Times have changed," said Uncle Alistair, and he stomped the sand from his boots. "It's 1927. The modern age! The days of digging wherever we want and shipping whatever we find out of Egypt to London or New York are over. About time, too. And unlike Ramses Faro, Feline Egyptologist, I choose to follow the rules."

"I follow the rules," the Feline Egyptologist said with a twitch of his whiskers. "Sometimes. Or rather..." He twitched his whiskers again. "Once. Possibly."

"You follow your own rules," Uncle Alistair said with a hearty laugh. "Always have, always will. Now...if you will excuse me, I have work to do. In the meantime, you may go to the temple." He winked at Felicity. "You *all* may go." He glanced at his niece's sketch of the blue crocodile on her sketchpad. "May I?"

She tore it off and handed it to her uncle. "Jolly fine work," he said as he went into his tent. "A perfect likeness." He poked his head out through the door again. "I say, old boy," he said to Ramses. "I should be ever so grateful if you do not lose or damage the children. And do please keep them away from the river. No telling what might be on the prowl tonight."

3

A crescent moon and surrounding stars bathed the broken temple walls in a light too dim for anyone but a cat to clearly see. Felicity held a lantern high before a carving of Sobek, the crocodile god. "The Sacred Crocodile Sleeps in the Reeds," she said, remembering the symbols on the little blue statue. "What do you think it means?"

"I shall guess 'the reeds' means a container of some kind," Ramses returned.

"And where might that be?"

"Somewhere nearby. In a secret chamber, unknown and undiscovered. I shall also guess a tomb robber dropped that crocodile centuries ago during a raid. How else would it have ended up out here, hidden until Sharrif tripped this morning?"

"Happy to help," Sharrif said again. He knew his friends were perfectly happy to spend hours trying to figure out the meaning of the reeds. He also knew he could be of no help at all. "I'll leave that to you," he said. "I'm going to explore on my own."

"Remember what Uncle Alistair told us," Felicity warned. "Don't go near the river."

"Don't worry," Sharrif said as he walked away from the lantern light. "I don't care much for Old Crocodile-Head." He pointed at the carving. "And I *really* don't care to meet one of his relatives."

Sharrif decided to explore an area he had not visited before. The sliver of moon lit the temple yard well enough to keep him from walking into the crazy jumble of tilted pillars and broken walls poking up through the sand. It also showed him something darker in the temple courtyard, a patch of black like a circular doorway cut into the earth.

Closer, he saw a staircase with two steps barely visible and a third disappearing down into utter darkness.

Did they lead to the secret chamber Ramses spoke of? He stepped down. "Hello?" A hollow echo returned the word in a dank whisper. *Hello-ello-ello.*

He liked the sound and tried it again. Another step down. "My name is Sharrif!" *Sharrif-arrif-arrif-arrif...*

He felt the step below with his sandal. Solid like the others, though he couldn't see it.

He stepped down to a fourth step and felt a chill in the air. "Must be close," he said, and *Close-ose-ose-ose* came the reply. He stepped down to the fifth and "no!" he realized - too late! - there was no fifth step.

He tried to pull back, but he had put too much weight forward. He couldn't stop. He reached for the wall – missed! He cried out when he tumbled into a pitch-black fall.

Bang! He slammed against a wall. *Scrape!* Up against another.

A second later, he plunged feet-first into a pool of filthy water. His right foot hit the bottom so hard he cried out in pain, but the water clapped over his head and muffled his cry.

He popped to the surface with a gasp. He tried to lift his right foot but it was wedged between two stones. Thankfully, the water only came up to his shoulders. (Any deeper, he would have drowned).

He looked from side to side but couldn't see a thing. When he looked up, he saw the entrance high above as a dark circle speckled with stars in the entirely black everything else. "A *well!*" he realized, though it was much larger than any other well he had ever seen, at least ten feet from one side to the other.

He pushed his hair from his eyes and called out: "Felicity!"

Felicity-icity-icity..

"Ramses!"

Amses-amses-amses-amses...

He called their names again and again but heard no answer. "Now what?" he asked so softly there came no echo in response.

But then something *did* respond.

He felt a ripple and heard a splash, and he nearly screamed when something squirmed past him.

He was not alone.

4

Uncle Alistair's tools lay against the temple wall, left there from their morning excavation. Felicity used one of the shovels to dig in the sand, hoping to find more about the blue crocodile. Ramses used his front paws to do the same beside her - *scratch-scratch-scritch-scratch*

"Find anything?" she asked.

"Only sand." *scritch-scritch-scratch-scri*...he stopped in mid-scritch and swiveled his ears. "What was that?"

"I didn't hear anything."

Ramses cocked his head. He swiveled his ears again and grew tense. "Something's wrong."

He dashed from the temple with Felicity following. When they reached the edge of the temple yard, Ramses stopped short. "Oh no...a Nilometer.*"

Felicity asked him what a Nilometer was, but all he said was, "That," and he pointed with the tip of his tail to a dark circle in the temple grounds surrounded by a low brick wall. Closer, they saw a tall stone that marked the entrance to a partial staircase leading down. Ramses hopped on the low wall and called. "Sharrif?" – *arrif-arrif-arrif.*

"Down here!" the boy called.

"Oh *no!*" Felicity cried, shocked to hear his voice from the black void.

She held the lantern over the gaping hole but could not see the bottom. "Are you all right?"

"Get me out!" Sharrif cried. "There's something down here. Ugh! It touched me!"

"We need a rope," Ramses said to Felicity.

"There's one at our camp. I'll get Uncle Alistair too."

"Wait – before you go." The cat peered into the darkness and called down to Sharrif. "When you say there's something down there, what might you mean?"

Sharrif said he didn't know, but whatever it was, it touched him again. "It's right beside me, I hear it splashing."

"Right then," Ramses muttered. "Desperate times call for desperate measures." He called again. "I'm going to drop down, Sharrif. Do try your best to catch me."

"I will."

"Promise?"

"I promise," said Sharrif.

"And I'll keep my claws in. Promise." Ramses noted Felicity's worried expression and said, "Can't leave him down there alone. After I take the plunge, you dash off and get your uncle and the rope. Oh…and my spectacles. Don't want to lose them in the leap." Felicity put his glasses in the pocket of her dress. He called down to Sharrif again. "Remember now. Catch me."

"I will."

Ramses nodded, and without another word, he hopped into the well. Falling feet first, he landed on Sharrif (who did not catch him) and tumbled into the water. "Well done," he said when he rose to the surface. He scrambled onto the boy's shoulder and shook his fur.

Sharrif wiped the droplets from his face. "Something's in here."

"Don't be afraid," Ramses whispered calmly in his ear. "I'm here with you."

"I'm going to our camp now," Felicity called from above.

"One moment more," Ramses said. "Hold the light up again."

Sharrif still couldn't see a thing, but the lantern's distant flame shed enough light for Ramses to see two tiny green eyes sparkling close to the wall. "It won't hurt us," he told Sharrif.

The eyes blinked. "And we won't hurt you," he said to the owner of the eyes.

"What is it?" Sharrif whispered.

"Crocodile." Before Sharrif could panic, the cat added: "A baby. Couldn't kill us if it tried, though I plan to keep my tail out of reach. You might do the same with your fingers."

Felicity called down again. "Should I go now?"

"Yes, go. And do make a dash for it. It's frightfully soggy down here."

5

Felicity's heart raced as she ran from the temple toward the light of their campfire. She planned to tell Uncle Alistair what happened, even if it made him angry (though Uncle Alistair never got truly angry.) On the other hand, if he learned of their friend's fall into the well, he might not let them explore on their own anymore. "I'll help Sharrif by myself," she thought.

Two tents stood near their crackling campfire. They used the first tent as their headquarters and Uncle Alistair's office. A lantern illuminated the canvas walls from within. The second tent, now dark, served as their living quarters. Felicity dashed inside this second one and opened a trunk near Sharrif's cot. A coil of rope lay amongst a jumble of tools. She slipped her arm through it and closed the lid.

When she stepped outside, she heard voices inside the first tent. Uncle Alistair was not alone. How peculiar! She approached without making a sound and leaned close.

Uncle Alistair's voice: "How many times – really how *many* times must I tell you? I don't know where it is, and I have no earthly idea what you mean by a 'key'. I know nothing more than you about this little blue chap."

Something didn't sound right. *He* didn't sound right. His voice was unusually tense.

Someone answered and the sound made her skin crawl.

She could not make out any words, only a low murmuring voice like the whisper of some awful, unwholesome creature living at the bottom of an abandoned well. This last thought brought her up short. A well! She would ask Uncle Alistair about his visitor later. Right now, she had to help Sharrif.

When she ran from their campsite, a shadow passed over the wall of Uncle Alistair's tent. The canvas door opened, but only by a narrow slit, enough to watch her leave…and then it closed again.

Felicity arrived back at the Nilometer and called down to her friends. "Can you climb out if I drop the rope?"

"My foot is caught," Sharrif said. "I can't move. And there's a crocodile down here."

"Crocodile!" Felicity exclaimed.

"It's a baby one, but I don't like baby crocodiles either."

Felicity held up the end of the rope. It was badly frayed. She wrapped it twice around the tall stone at the top of the staircase and tied it with one of the knots Uncle Alistair taught her.

She tested it – perfectly tight.

"Cover your head." She dropped the rope. It splashed into the water beside Sharrif. "Can you reach it?"

"Yes." He felt his right foot with his left. "My foot...it's jammed between something. Two stones, maybe part of the floor."

"I'm coming down," Felicity said. "But I need to find something first." She raced to the place where they found the blue crocodile. She scattered their excavation tools until she found a short flat piece of iron Uncle Alistair used to separate bricks from their mortar.

Back at the Nilometer, she hauled the rope back up, tied the lantern to its end, and lowered it again.

Sharrif held the lantern high, but instead of looking up at her, he focused on the little reptile floating nearby. It was about eighteen inches long from the tip of its snout to the tip of its ridged tail. It stared at him with green eyes and appeared far more curious than dangerous.

Felicity took off her shoes and dropped the iron bar into a second pocket of her blue dress (she didn't want to crack Ramses' spectacles in the first). She shimmied down the rope. "Ugh, this water," she said when her foot touched the surface. "It's so..." She couldn't find the words.

"Wet," Ramses suggested.

"Much worse than wet." She lowered further, sinking until her bare feet touched the slimy bottom. "This is awful. How in the world...?"

"I thought it might lead to a tomb," Sharrif said.

"It's not a tomb, it's a Nilometer," Felicity returned as if she knew what a Nilometer was. "Which is...you tell him," she said to Ramses. While Felicity felt the floor around Sharrif's feet with her own, Ramses pointed out a series of chiseled marks on the walls. "It's used to measure the height of the river during the annual floods. Lucky for us those floods haven't come this year." He asked Felicity for his spectacles. After she set them on his head, he adjusted them with his paws and studied the brick walls of the well…rough and easily climbed near the water, but too smooth to use his claws beyond that.

"You're right," Felicity said to Sharrif. "Your foot is jammed between two stones. This is what we'll do." She shuddered. "I'm going to try to pry them apart with this iron bar. You hold the lantern. If it goes out while we're down here…" She shuddered again and took a deep breath and dropped into the filthy black water. With her eyes tightly closed, she felt around the ooze and muck until she found Sharrif's foot. She wedged the iron bar between the stones and pulled. Sharrif slipped his foot from his sandal.

She rose to the surface and brushed the water from her eyes. "Can you stand on it?"

"It hurts, but it's not broken," Sharrif said.

He pushed at his sandal until it broke free and floated to the surface. "I think those stones made it feel worse than it is."

Ramses finished his study of the walls. "The rope is the only way out."

"I'll go first," Felicity said. She grabbed the rope with both hands and pulled on it, fully expecting to haul herself from the water. Instead, she fell back against Sharrif. The rope quivered and fell and dropped over them in a tangle. "What in the world…?"

"Did you tie it tight?" Sharrif asked.

"I'm sure I did!" Felicity pulled the rope hand over fist to the end. "Ramses, look."

He stared at the end of the rope, no longer frayed.
"Cut."

6

"Now what?" Felicity asked.

"Your Uncle will come," Ramses said from his perch on

Sharrif's shoulder. "Eventually." He looked up at the smooth sides of the well. "Won't he?"

"I didn't tell him," Felicity admitted. "I thought we might get in trouble."

"And behold. You were right."

"Why would someone cut the rope?" Sharrif asked. "And *who* would do it? We're alone here."

"No, we're not." Felicity told them about the sinister voice she heard in the tent. "Someone was with him. They must have done this."

"But why?" Sharrif asked again.

No one had an answer. They inspected the walls and searched for a hidden doorway, but no luck.

"We'll have to wait for Uncle Alistair to notice we're gone," Felicity said. "Knowing him, he won't do that until morning when he's noticed no one has made tea. We may have to stay down here all night."

"What if the lamp runs out of oil?" Sharrif asked and Felicity groaned at the thought. The filthy water reached six inches below her shoulders and even closer to Sharrif's (she was two inches taller). It dripped from her braids and the boy's long black hair. Ramses was soaking wet in spite of several vigorous fur-shakes.

The baby crocodile made a chirping sound.

"At least it's not fully grown," Felicity said. "Imagine if…" She paused, staring at the little reptile. "Wait a minute." She handed the lantern to Sharrif and waded up close to the baby crocodile. "How did *you* get in here?"

"Excellent question," Ramses said. He tapped Sharrif with his paw and asked him to carry him over. "Now see here, mate," he said to the crocodile. "We're in a bit of a pickle. Did you drop down from above like we did?"

The crocodile croaked.

"Is that a no?"

It chirped.

"A chirp is a yes and a croak is a no?" Ramses asked.

chirp.

"So, there must be another way, yes?"

chirp.

The crocodile lifted its head from the water and pointed its snout at a dark shadow upon the brick wall. It swam around Felicity, stopped in front of her, and pointed again.

"What's he saying?" Felicity asked. "Are you a he?"

chirp

"It's a boy crocodile."

"Lift him," Ramses said.

"Lift the crocodile?" she asked. Ramses nodded and Felicity gingerly grasped the reptile around his middle and lifted him closer to the shadow on the wall.

"Now do the same with me," Ramses said to Sharrif.

The boy lifted him, and the cat and the crocodile hung side by side with their tails dangling and dripping. "There's an opening," Ramses said. "Those rough bricks hid it. Might it lead us out of here?"

chirp.

"It may be a tunnel, leading from here to the river," Ramses said. "That's how our little leathery friend got in here. If we can enlarge that opening, and you two can fit, it may lead us to freedom. If not, I'll go alone and fetch your uncle."

They used the iron bar to pry four bricks from their mortar and make an opening large enough for Felicity and Sharrif to squirm through. Ramses went first. "I was right, it *is* a tunnel."

The little crocodile floated up close to Felicity. "Don't worry, we won't leave you," she said. "If it hadn't been for you, we'd have been down here all night."

chirp.

After she lifted the crocodile into the passageway, Sharrif hoisted himself up. She handed him the lantern and followed. Before them lay a pitch-black tunnel about three feet high and three feet wide, with no end in sight. The air within was heavy and stale.

Felicity didn't like the look of it at all. "Are you sure this leads outside?"

Ramses looked at the crocodile. "Does it?"

With another chirp, the little crocodile scrambled into the tunnel. He stopped and looked back like a puppy making sure its owner was following.

"And on we go?" Ramses asked.

"And on we go," Felicity returned with a reluctant sigh.

Before long, the narrow tunnel opened into a larger space. Sharrif lifted the lantern. "Look at that!" he said, and their eyes widened with surprise.

They had entered a hidden underground chamber with its walls and ceiling covered with paintings as rich and detailed as a royal tomb. Broken pieces of wood and shattered pottery littered the floor.

"Raided long ago," Ramses said. "This must be part of the temple complex." He looked up at the ceiling. "Paintings of Sobek. I wonder who built it." He lowered his gaze to the relief carvings on the wall. "Ah there," he said. "A cartouche*."

"What's a cartouche?" Sharrif asked, hoping if it might be another word for "exit".

"Over there, that frame," Felicity said to Sharrif, and she nodded at one of the walls and an oval frame with hieroglyphic characters inside. "They always surround a pharaoh's name." She pointed out some of the symbols inside: a flowering reed, an owl, and the front half of a lion with paws outstretched. "This one reads…" She hesitated, mouthing some words silently. "I think it says 'Amun*…is…in front'." She turned to the expert. "Is it?"

"Quite right," Ramses said. "The pharaoh's birth name. Amun is in front. The hieroglyphs read *Imn-h-ha.t,* or as we've come to know him, Amenemhat III.*" Ramses cocked his head, puzzled. "Amenemhat III," he repeated, "who should not be here at all. Kom Ombo was built long, long after his reign. Unless…"

"Maybe this part is older than the temple above?" Felicity suggested.

"Possibly," Ramses returned, "but it would have to be much older. Well over a thousand years."

"What's an Amun*?" Sharrif asked.

"Not a what," Felicity said. "A who. A creator god. When Amun shows himself, he comes as a sphinx* with a ram's head."

"I don't know how you two can keep all those gods and pharaohs straight," Sharrif said.

"I don't know them all," Felicity admitted. "I only know the major pharaohs like this one. Amenemhat III. Eleventh – no, Twelfth Dynasty*."

Again, Sharrif shook his head. "Like that! They're all the same to me. All dead and dusty and…" He froze, staring straight ahead with an expression of alarm so intense it passed to Felicity and clutched at her heart, though she had no idea why.

"Look," Sharrif whispered. He pointed across the chamber.

Felicity turned and nearly screamed at the sight of three massive crocodiles hulking in the shadows.

"Well, well, well…" Ramses said quietly, and he shocked them when he bounded toward the beasts with a hearty shout: "How do you do, my fine fellows?"

"Ramses don't!" Felicity cried.

"Fear not!" He hopped onto the head of the nearest crocodile. "You see? Harmless."

Felicity and Sharrif moved closer and saw the three figures were, in fact, crocodile mummies.

Their hides had long since dried into black leather and the linen wrappings that once covered them from snout to tail hung about them in blackened tatters.

"Why would anyone want a crocodile mummy?" Sharrif asked with his hand over his still-beating heart. Ramses told him they were sacred to the god Sobek. "Old Crocodile-Head," the boy said with a frown. "If *he* shows up, I will faint dead away. I really will."

"No danger of that," Ramses said. He gazed at the ceiling again. "I don't understand the purpose of this place. Why so hidden away? And why the mummies?"

"Was it a tomb?" Felicity asked.

"Not for Amenemhat III. His tomb is five hundred miles north of here in the Faiyum Oasis*." He pawed at a piece of broken pottery. "Looted long ago, whatever it was."

Felicity touched one of the crocodile mummies, hard as stone. Lifting her eyes, she saw a small box lying beside it, empty, with its lid half open. "What's this?" She stepped over the crocodile and picked it up. "Ramses, look."

He hopped onto the mummy and strolled down the length of its ridged tail. Felicity set the box down so he could see it. It looked like a miniature sarcophagus with its lid carved to look like a bundle of reeds. Ramses crouched beside it with a satisfied purr. "The Sacred Crocodile Sleeps in the Reeds…might this be the reeds?"

"Looks like someone pried it open with a knife," Felicity said.

Ramses looked inside. "I suspect this once contained the little blue crocodile."

"*Our* little blue crocodile?" Sharrif asked.

Ramses nodded. "Stolen by the same shameless thieves who took everything else."

Felicity closed the sarcophagus lid. When she did, Ramses leaned in close.

Labyrinth of the Crocodiles

He used his paw to push his glasses closer to his eyes and the same paw to wipe the dust from a line of hieroglyphs carved into the lid. He froze suddenly, tense, the same way he did when spotting a mouse.

"What is it?" Felicity asked. "Do you see something?"

Ramses did not take his eyes from the lid. "We must bring it to your uncle."

"Why?" she asked. "What does it say?"

"Wherein Lies the Key to the Labyrinth of the Crocodiles," he said in a voice little more than a whisper.

Sharrif shrugged. "Whatever that is. How do we get out of here?"

"This way," Ramses said. He led them across the chamber to a second tunnel similar to the first. "I smell water. I have since we first set foot in this place. I expect we'll come out on the riverbank. Be watchful." He nodded at the baby crocodile. "Don't want to run into little leathery friend's Mum."

After they crawled into the second tunnel, the lantern light faded and the three crocodile mummies once more lay in their eternal darkness. They stayed like that, too, when Ramses and his companions emerged from the tunnel into fresh air and starlight, and the three crocodiles mummies remained behind, silent, and utterly still, as they had for over three thousand years…

…and then one of them shuddered

…and another one stirred and moved its tail

…and the one closest to the escape tunnel opened its blank and lifeless eyes.

7

Ramses popped out of the tunnel onto a part of the riverbank well-hidden from passing boats and curious travelers. The baby crocodile followed. When he saw the moonlight shining on the river, he scrambled over the sand and plopped into the water.

"Is he gone?" Sharrif asked when he emerged from the tunnel. "I didn't have a chance to say good-bye." He seemed a little disappointed, which surprised Felicity. "Why would you want to?" she asked. "You hate crocodiles."

"I kind of liked this one," Sharrif said. He waved at the river. "Bye little croc." Two tiny eyes appeared on the surface and sparkled in the lantern light. It looked like he was waiting for them to join him.

"Sorry, mate," Ramses called. "Our place is on land." The crocodile chirped but would not leave. "Suit yourself," the cat said, and he suggested Felicity and Sharrif move further up the riverbank. "Think about his lovely Mum, and how thrilled we'd be to never make her acquaintance. Now then...we need to find out who cut that rope."

Felicity held up the reed sarcophagus. "And we need to show this to Uncle Alistair."

"Right-o," Ramses said. "But first, I'd like to sniff about for a moment or two."

"We'll come with you," Felicity said.

"Not yet. This requires slinking and skulking."

"I can slink," she insisted.

"Skulk too," added Sharrif.

"You can, yes, but I'd rather you stay here," Ramses said. "Give me ten minutes and then join me at the Nilometer." As he turned to leave, he glanced at the tunnel entrance. He did not see anything, but he felt a sudden tingle along his spine that made the fur on his back rise. He stared at the gaping black hole. "I'd rather you not go near the tunnel either," he said, and he vanished into the reeds.

"Honestly, you'd think we were four years old," Felicity said after he disappeared. "Uncle Alistair never wants us to do anything. Ramses wants us to do everything, but then he never lets us do it." She thought for a moment and admitted, "Well, yes, he does let us do most things, but not *everything*. I can slink and skulk."

"I can too," Sharrif said before confessing he had no idea if he'd ever slinked or skulked in his life and wasn't entirely certain he knew what slinking and skulking were all about.

"They're like sneaking," Felicity said. "And yes, fine. Ramses can sneak without making a sound."

"And he can see in the dark," Sharrif said.

"True."

"And he can get in and out of really small holes."

"Also true," Felicity admitted.

"And he hears better than anyone with those big ears."

"Also true."

"And he can squirm like an eel when someone grabs him."

Felicity weakened. "Fine, all right, fine. He's a better skulker, slinker, and sneaker, but I still want to try." A rustle in the dry reeds distracted her. "Oh no, go back. Go away!"

The little crocodile had climbed out of the water. They tried to coax him back, but he would not budge.

Sharrif scooped the reptile up into his arms. "I don't like crocodiles, but I think you'd make a nice pet until you get big enough to eat us. Can we keep him?"

Felicity patted their new friend on the head. "You think we should?"

"We can't send him back into the river alone," Sharrif said. "Ramses says his lovely Mum might be around, but we haven't seen her. Maybe he's lost. Or maybe he's an orphan like us."

"I don't know," Felicity said, thinking of Uncle Alistair's reaction.

"We can't send him back," Sharrif insisted. "He might get lost. He might die! He'll be our pet."

Felicitys nodded. "We would have to name him. I think he looks like a Gerald."

"Gerald!" Sharrif frowned. "But he's Egyptian, same as me and Ramses. He should have an Egyptian name."

"Good point," Felicity said. "What is the Arabic word for crocodile?"

"*Timsah.*"

"What do you think of Timsah?" she asked the crocodile and he chirped and that was that: he became their pet, and Timsah was his name.

8

Skulking and slinking, Ramses crept over the sand to the Nilometer. He twitched his whiskers and sniffed the air.

sniff

...smoke from their campfire.

sniff-sniff

...filthy water in the Nilometer. Faint trace of boot leather, very faint.

sniff sniff sniff

...mouse hiding nearby. Tempting, but no time for that now.

He inspected the end of the rope still tied around the stone and sliced through with a knife. Who would cut it? And why?

He studied the footprints in the sand.

He saw tracks made by Sharrif and Felicity, and other tracks made by a man's boots. They did not belong to Jammpot. He would recognize Jammpot's boot prints anywhere, and these were not his.

They were far too large.

They were absolutely massive.

He remembered what Felicity said earlier: *"Someone in the tent with Uncle Alistair."*

He swiveled his ears at the sound of an automobile engine starting, somewhere distant. He shook his whiskers and sniffed again. More smoke. But no…wait. This was something more than smoke from a campfire.

A flickering glow appeared above the palm trees.

"Something wrong," he whispered, and he dashed into the palm grove. The smoke grew thicker. The light burned brighter. When he sprang from the grove, he slid to a halt at the sight of a fire whipping up from the back of the office tent.

He leapt over the much smaller campfire. "Jammpot!" he called. No one answered.

He poked his head inside the burning tent and squinted. No Jammpot. A lantern lay on its side near the back. Its spilled oil had set the fire.

Jammpot's chair lay upended on the floor. His papers lay scattered around it. Ramses hopped onto the desk. Felicity's sketch of the little blue crocodile lay upon it but the crocodile itself was not there. He was about to leap for the door when he noticed a mark on the desk, a spill of ink, but one made with a fingertip on purpose.

A second kerosene lamp exploded. Drops of flame spattered over the unburned walls.

Ramses sprang through the front door at the same moment Felicity and Sharrif emerged from the palm grove, wide-eyed and out of breath. "Where's Uncle Alistair?" Felicity called.

"Not in there," Ramses returned. "I'll go look for him. Be back in a jiff!" he said, and he bounded off into the desert.

Felicity pointed to the second tent. "Look!" Tatters of blazing canvas from the first tent had set the second one on fire.

Sharrif held the baby crocodile close to his chest. "What'll we do?"

"Everything we have is in there," Felicity cried. "But that won't matter if I can get..." She did not finish the thought, but Sharrif knew what she meant.

"You're not going *in* there!" he said. She set the lantern and the reed sarcophagus down beside the campfire. "Felicity, you can't!" he insisted.

"It hasn't spread too far yet." As soon as she said it, the poles holding up the first tent collapsed into a spiral of sparks. "No time," she said, and she ran into the second tent.

She raced to Uncle Alistair's cot and pulled a small key from under the right front leg. She used it to open a steamer trunk at the foot of the same cot.

"Felicity!" she heard.

"Coming!" She rummaged inside the trunk. "Where *is* it?" she whispered, frantic.

Fire crackled upon the ceiling, brightening as it came.

She turned one of her uncle's desert boots upside-down. A leather purse fell onto the floor.

Flames broke through the canvas with a roar. "Got it!" she said when she ran out of the tent with the purse, wiping her eyes and coughing. "Where's Ramses?" she asked. "Did he come back?"

"He did," the cat said at the edge of the firelight. She could not tell by his stern gaze if he was annoyed or impressed…probably a little of both. "Someone was here with a vehicle," he said. "I heard it leave. Your uncle went with them."

"Why?" Felicity asked, bewildered. "He would never leave our campsite on fire like this. He wouldn't leave without telling us."

"I didn't say he went willingly."

"You mean someone *took* him?" She thought of her uncle's strength and his trim, muscular frame. He was not the sort to be taken against his will.

"Come," Ramses said. "I'll show you."

Behind their camp, they found the marks and signs of a great disturbance. Tire tracks. Boot prints. Something heavy pulled across the sand. Ramses touched one of the boot prints with his right paw.

It belonged to Jammpot. He touched another print and recognized that one too. They were the same enormous boot prints he saw back at the Nilometer. Whoever owned them had cut the rope. He came to a mass of confused tracks and saw Jammpot's leading away from the tire track.

He had tried to escape. Two long grooves beside the tracks showed that someone had caught him and dragged him back. Someone big. Someone more than big – someone *enormous*.

He hopped from footprint to footprint, following Jammpot's attempted escape. "Look at this," he said, and Felicity and Sharrif joined him, carrying Timsah

Ramses crouched beside a mark in the sand, staring at it. Like the ink in the tent, it was made by a finger. "Tell me again what you heard in the tent."

Felicity crouched beside him. "I heard Uncle Alistair say he didn't know where it was...though I didn't hear him say what *it* might be. I think I heard something about a key."

"And the other voice?" Ramses asked.

"No words I could make out, but the sound..." Felicity shuddered. "Low and sort of whispery, like hissing but not hissing...oh, I can't describe it."

Ramses stared at the mark upon the ground. "The low scrape of sand across a lonely dune."

Felicity nodded. Something in the cat's voice worried her.

Ramses touched the mark with his paw. "Your uncle left this for us. A clue. He did the same with ink on his desk. He expected us to find it."

Felicity raised the lantern higher.

Its glow highlighted the ridges in the sand.

"The first mark could have been an accident," Ramses said. "This second one is not. He meant to tell us the identity of someone I hoped to never again see in any of my nine lives." Before they could ask who, the cat stepped away from the mark and said, "We must find your uncle and we must do so quickly. The less time he spends with her, the better..."

"Her?" Felicity repeated, and her heart was in her throat though she did not know why.

"Yes, *her*," Ramses said, and he gazed out to where the tire tracks faded into darkness and the moon settled low upon the dunes. "The Countess, Serpentina von Hyss."

Ramses Faro

II.

THE ROSE AND VENOM

A Jammpot – Temple at Karnak

Ramses Faro

1

Felicity barely remembered her parents. She knew what they looked like: a portrait in the study of their rented villa in Cairo showed her mother to be tall and slender, like Felicity, with the same light brown hair and hazel eyes. Her father was a dashing fighter pilot with a sleek black mustache like his younger brother Alistair. Felicity was only two years old when his plane was shot down during the Great War. Later that year, her mother fell victim to the Spanish Flu.

Now an orphan, she spent her early childhood in a gloomy, drafty London townhouse under the care of her father's elder sister, Ludmilla-Florence Jammpot.

Aunt Ludmilla-Florence Jammpot disliked children. She considered them to be loud and unnecessary, and she was secretly relieved when her youngest brother Alistair decided to bring Felicity to Egypt when she was seven years old. Aunt Ludmilla-Florence would never admit this, of course. She pretended to be outraged that her brother would dare steal the girl away from the comforts of rainy, grey London.

"Steal her, don't be ridiculous Ludmilla, of course I didn't steal her," Uncle Alistair insisted over a crackling telephone at the steamship dock. "I borrowed her. And besides, it was her idea. Quite impossible to say no."

They went back and forth until Aunt Ludmilla-Florence began to worry her brother might do the only thing worse than taking Felicity away, which was to bring her back.

She agreed to let the girl go provided she be given a proper education. Uncle Alistair agreed. He promised to enroll her in the Classical Academy in Cairo under the leadership of Master Theodorus (though he did not tell her Master Theodorus was an owl). "And furthermore," droned Aunt Ludmilla-Florence, "I absolutely forbid you to take her on one of your pointless adventures with that beastly feline." (She had never forgiven Ramses for attacking her favorite feathered hat.)

"Wouldn't dream of it," said Alistair, but within hours of the steamship's arrival in Egypt, he joined a camel caravan heading into the western desert with the beastly feline perched upon his shoulder and Felicity seated behind him, clinging to his jacket. "Thought you would never dream of taking your niece on a pointless, ridiculous adventure," Ramses said to his particular friend.

"And I wouldn't," Uncle Alistair returned with a sly grin. "I dream of things like flying hyenas and chatting with a pot of marmalade. I have never once dreamt of riding on a camel with you and Felicity. If and when I do, I shall alert my sister. Until then - on we go!"

Felicity adored her uncle. He was kind-hearted, adventurous, scatter-brained, brilliant, and most of all, endlessly fun. He was devilishly handsome too (something he seemed completely unaware of and never acknowledged), and the ladies loved him. He was the one who invited Sharrif to become a part of their family and join them on their travels — the same as he did with Ramses years earlier. They were a close little band of adventurers and now, his kidnapping at the hands of the mysterious Countess von Hyss distressed Felicity to no end. "How will we find him?" she now asked. "And where?"

Ramses pawed at the squiggle they found in the sand. "The *how* we do not yet know. I suspect the *where* is in the city of Luxor, near the Temple of Karnak. The Countess owns a shop there called The Rose and Venom where she deals in stolen and fake antiquities."

"How did she know about our excavation site here, and the blue crocodile?" Felicity asked.

"I think I know," Sharrif offered. "Remember when your uncle said he contacted the Museum?" He pointed past the smoldering tents toward the tiny village of Ombos. "I saw a telegraph office when we first arrived. Someone might have listened in. How far is Luxor from here?"

"Ninety miles north," Ramses said. "We could go by boat."

Sharrif studied the smoke rising from the tents in straight columns. "No wind tonight. And who knows when the next steamboat might pass?"

"I saw no motorcars in Ombos," Felicity said. "Only dust and donkeys."

"Camels too," Sharrif said. "If we hire a big, strong one, we could get to Luxor in a single day. But not if it's a talkative one. Talkative camels are too slow. They like to point things out."

Felicity lifted the purse she found in the trunk. "We have enough to hire a camel. We could hire five if we wanted."

"We only need one to carry us all, including him," Ramses said, and he nodded at the baby crocodile still nestled in Sharrif's arms. "*If* you decide to keep him. Do you?"

Sharrif and Felicity both said yes at the same time.

"What do you have to say about it, little leathery friend?" Ramses asked. The crocodile chirped his version of "yes", though not right away, and not very loud. When Ramses told him there was still time to back out, he said nothing at all.

2

Sharrif volunteered to find a camel. When Felicity offered to go with him, he glanced at Ramses. The cat knew at once the boy had silently told him to agree with whatever he was about to say. "I have a lot of experience haggling with camel merchants," Sharrif said. "I might have to convince the camel too. It's better if I go on my own."

Before she could object, Ramses said, "A fine idea! Meanwhile, Felicity and I can look for something of use that escaped the fire."

Felicity shrugged. "How much to hire a camel?"

"I don't need money yet," Sharrif replied.

"Of course, you do," Felicity said. "Unless you plan on taking one without paying."

Sharrif glanced at Ramses again. "Right-o!" the cat exclaimed, changing the subject. "How long will it take?"

"Not long at all." Sharrif handed the baby crocodile to Felicity. "I'll be back in a jiff," he said to Timsah and he turned on his heels. Within seconds, his black robe melted into the night.

"Well, that was peculiar," Felicity said as she watched him go. "Sharrif is awfully peculiar at times, don't you think?"

"As are we all," Ramses said. "I hope we are anyway. Nothing worse than someone who is never peculiar."

They searched the campsite but found little that survived apart from Felicity's sketchpad and pencil left beside the campfire earlier that night.

They decided to look over the excavation tools back at the temple to see if any might be worth taking.

"The Countess," Felicity said on the way through the palms. "Who is she?"

"Serpentina von Hyss," Ramses said with a shudder. "Claims to be German nobility, though I have my doubts. What I do *not* doubt is that she is a nasty piece of work if ever there was one."

"Is she strong enough to force Uncle Alistair into a motor car?"

"Not at all." Ramses chuckled at the thought. "She couldn't force a fly into a car. But her manservant, he is a different story altogether. Pickelhaube."

"Pickel...?"

"Haube," Ramses repeated. "Major Hermann-Düüfus von Pickelhaube, formerly of the Imperial German Army. A monstrosity of a man, but silent as a stone. Devoted to Countess von Hyss. Never leaves her side. Most of all, if there is any seriously awful business to perform, Pickelhaube is the one to do it."

A bird called when they arrived at the temple, *toc toc churrrrrrrrr.*

"Egyptian nightjar," Felicity said.

They inspected their excavation tools, but found nothing worth taking, apart from a knife. "Better to travel light," Ramses said. He looked up at Felicity. "Speaking of which...."

She caught his meaning and held Timsah closer. "He wants to come with us."

"Let's give him one more chance to decide."

They crossed the temple courtyard to the riverbank where Felicity set the little reptile down on the sand. When Timsah saw the moonlight on the river, he chirped and moved toward it...and stopped again. He spun around and perched upon the top of Felicity's shoe. "That settles that," she said.

Ramses strolled up to the crocodile. "Now see here, old brick. There is no telling what we're getting ourselves into. Could be a spot of trouble ahead." He nodded at the slow-moving water. "Now is your chance. What say you?"

The crocodile looked up at Felicity and back at Ramses but did not move.

"Very well," the cat said. "We made the offer, and you…" He froze, with his gaze nailed upon the water's edge.

"What is it?" Felicity whispered. She scooped the little crocodile into her arms.

Ramses didn't answer. He crept down the riverbank without making a sound. There, he found three wide grooves, as if something heavy had been dragged over the sand. He followed the grooves with his eyes and saw they led from the tunnel to the river. "These must have been here before," he thought, puzzled. "I didn't notice them, that's all. Someone must have hauled three small boats over the sand." He started to turn but hesitated once more, staring at the grooves. "That must be it," he thought. "What else could they be?"

"I wonder how Sharrif is getting on," Felicity said when they returned to their charred campsite with the crocodile Timsah. After gazing into the darkness where she last caught sight of her friend, she said, "Don't tell him I said this."

"Wouldn't dream of it," Ramses returned.

"Cross your whiskers and hope to die?"

Ramses swept his right front paw over his whiskers on both sides of his face. "Promise."

"He doesn't care about hieroglyphs or pharaohs or the things we like," Felicity said. "Do you think he's happy?"

"Seems perfectly happy to me."

"Happy with us, I mean. Me and you and Uncle Alistair. He doesn't like school. He doesn't get along with Master Theodorus."

"Neither did I," Ramses said.

"Master Theodorus says you were the best student in the entire history of the Academy."

"Which is a surprise, coming from that old bird. I did all right, I suppose, but I caused my share of trouble. More than my share. Breaking that priceless Greek vase." He raised his eyebrow whiskers. "That was quite an episode. Knocking over the candle into the papyrus collection was too. And then the mouse in science class."

"Set it loose?"

"Ate it."

"Sharrif would never do any of those things," Felicity admitted. "Especially the mouse part. But he's having a hard time in his classes."

"You think he'd be better off where we found him?"

"No!" Felicity said, and she surprised herself by how strongly she said it. "I mean…no. I don't think that at all."

"He seemed to enjoy his life at the monastery."

"But he also seemed to enjoy leaving it to come stay with us."

"And now?"

"I don't think the things that interest us interest him," she said. "Do you?"

"Possibly not."

"I wish they did," Felicity added after a pause. "I think he'd be so much happier."

"Why would you ever think such a thing?" Ramses asked.

"Because…" She paused again as if she, too, suddenly wondered why she would ever think such a thing. She shrugged and said, "Because who wouldn't like Egyptology?"

Ramses perked up and swiveled his ears. "Quiet now," he whispered. "He's here."

Felicity peered into the darkness but saw only shadows, but then the darkness moved, and a figure loomed out of the black.

"Sharrif!" she said, and her friend saluted her from atop the largest camel she had ever seen.

"And on we go!" he said, and the camel snorted and rolled his eyes and muttered something nasty under his breath.

3

The camel (who refused to tell Sharrif his name) wore a sturdy saddle over a multi-colored woolen blanket and a halter of rope wrapped in blue cloth. Felicity was certain that such a magnificent beast used up a good deal of their money. "How much did he cost?"

"Do you see a price tag?" the camel asked with a sneer.

Felicity apologized. "I meant the price to hire you."

"As if it's your business," the camel said, and he snorted again.

What an annoying camel! "What's your name?" she asked.

Sharrif swung his leg over the saddle and dropped the long drop from the saddle to the sand. "He won't tell me."

The nameless camel stomped his foot and grumbled. "I might as well say it now. It's none of your business."

"What isn't?" Felicity asked.

He stared down his nose: "Whatever you want to know."

"He's awfully grumpy," Sharif said. "But he's strong. And fast. Strong and fast are more important than non-grumpy for desert travel."

Felicity reached into the purse. "Which brings me back to this. How much?"

"None of your business."

"I wasn't asking you," she said to the grumpy camel, and she repeated the question to Sharrif.

"Nothing yet," Sharrif replied.

She eyed him suspiciously. "You didn't…" She almost said "steal" but the word was too strong, too direct. "You didn't take him, did you?"

"As Ramses says, desperate times call for desperate measures," Sharrif reminded her. "No camel merchant would hire out one of his beasts to a boy or girl or, especially, a cat."

The camel stomped his front foot again. "Oh, that's rich, a beastly boy calling me a beast," he grumbled to himself. "Will this nightmare never end?"

"And I didn't *take* him," Sharrif continued. "I opened the gate and let all the donkeys and camels loose. It will take the merchant three days to round them up. In the meantime, we'll take this one to Luxor."

"For the 'special' thing," said the camel, "if such a thing exists, which I doubt it does."

"A carrot," Sharrif said. He told the others the grumpy camel had never tasted a carrot before. He had never seen one. "After we get to Luxor and find some carrots, we'll put a few coins in the saddlebag and send Grumpy home before anyone notices he's gone."

"Splendid work," Ramses said and turned to Felicity. "Wouldn't you agree?"

She nodded and smiled and dropped the purse into her pocket. "I would."

Ramses and the Jammpots met Sharrif the year before on an earlier adventure in the north of Egypt. Unlike Felicity, who had a vague memory of her mother and father, Sharrif never knew his parents at all. He was abandoned as a newborn baby on the doorstep of the desert monastery of St. Macarius and he grew up there, well-loved, and well-cared for. He looked after the camels and donkeys and was known as "the camel-boy Sharrif" (even after the Abbot bestowed his own last name upon him and called him Sharrif Aziz).

He lived in the stable by choice and spent many long evenings in deep conversation with his friends, especially the camels. He had other jobs too. He fixed things that needed to be fixed. He tended to the fig trees. He repaired mud brick walls. He accompanied the supply boat to Cairo and eventually learned to sail it himself. It was a good and easy life, but Sharrif had a spirit of adventure he did not know he possessed until he met Ramses and the Jammpots.

They had stopped at the monastery on their way to Alexandria. Felicity told him of their various journeys, and they were the most exciting stories Sharrif had ever heard. He begged the Abbot to allow him to go with them. The Abbot agreed, and when Uncle Alistair later suggested the boy attend school in Cairo, the monks agreed to that too.

They were sad, but they knew a life beyond the monastery walls was a better fit for an adventuresome boy.

It *was* a better fit, but his experience with school was not. He struggled. He spoke English and Arabic, but he could not read either one very well. Hieroglyphs were impossible.

Where did he belong? He had no adventures in the monastery, but he was useful. Now he had adventures, but often felt useless. Sometimes he even felt stupid. Felicity, Ramses and Uncle Alistair never called him stupid (they would never dream of saying such a thing) but his teachers had no reluctance.

They were owls, all of them. Some were kind. Some were not. Some were young. Most were not.

"If you would only *try*, young Sharrif," Master Theodorus would say after a weary hoot. "If you would make an effort, you might come within striking distance of a correct answer."

And that was the trouble. Sharrif *did* try.

He studied longer than the others. He took more notes. He tried to focus on his books instead of daydreaming or gazing out the window. Nothing worked.

His classmates could rattle off the names of pharaohs simply by looking at the hieroglyphic symbols. To Sharrif they all looked like pictures. Beetles. Feathers. Snakes. Falcons. He could not find a single pharaoh's name among them. And then there were the dynasties, the gods, and the Old Kingdom and New Kingdom, which was still extremely old. Confusing!

Still, there were things he could do the others could not. He could fix the broken hinge on the classroom door. He figured out what was wrong with the hand pump at the well. He replaced a pane of glass broken years before by a certain student named R. Faro, and he certainly knew how to talk to a camel better than anyone else. He knew how to handle one too.

"This is what we'll do," he now said. "We'll travel most of this night and sleep for a couple hours before the sun comes up. We'll have a long, hot day tomorrow, but we'll get through it. I put some waterskins in the saddlebag. We'll fill those along the way." He grabbed the camel by the halter. "You're going to be good and do as I ask."

"No."

"Carrot."

"I meant yes."

"We need to climb aboard now." The camel wrinkled his upper lip and glared at the boy. Sharrif shook his halter. "Carrot," he said again. Grumpy bellowed with irritation, "Misery, all is misery," and sank to his knees. When Felicity reached for the saddle, he added: "Hope you don't weigh as much as you look."

She ignored him and climbed aboard. After Sharrif helped her get settled, he handed up Timsah, climbed onto the saddle, and sat in front of Felicity with Ramses between them. "Hang on," he said, and he tapped his heels into the camel's hide.

Up went the beast with another bellowing groan, and they rose nearly eight feet into the air. "Which way?" the camel asked.

"North," said Sharrif. "To Luxor."

4

They skirted around the village of Ombos to avoid the camel's owner and passed into a sugarcane field under a sky ablaze with stars. They gazed at them in wonder and silence until they were well past the village. When they finally decided it was safe to have a conversation, they found it wasn't easy.

Whenever they tried to talk about Uncle Alistair or the sacred blue crocodile or the reed sarcophagus, the grumpy camel would snort and say, "Nonsense," or "A likely story," or, his favorite, "Rubbish. Balderdash and rubbish." Eventually, even he got tired of his unpleasant ways, and he let them carry on a whispered conversation as they passed through the last of the sugarcane fields.

Felicity and Sharrif wanted to learn more about Timsah. They made a game of it by asking questions to get a chirp or a croak in reply, and in this way discovered many things about their new friend.

He was hatched on a sandbank across the river from Kom Ombo.

A stork nearly ate him when he was three days old.

Sometime later a mongoose chased him and he escaped into the tunnel beneath the temple, which was how he ended up in the Nilometer.

He didn't trust dragonflies.

He had never tasted a fig.

He missed his family, but he had a new family now.

When they asked about the new family, Felicity and Sharrif were delighted to realize he meant them. And Ramses too, of course.

"We're a family of friends!" Felicity said with a joyful laugh. "We thought about calling you our pet, but you're not a pet," she said to Timsah. "Uncle Alistair doesn't like the word 'pet'. None of us do, so you're not a pet. You're a friend."

"Oh, how very touching," said the camel with a snort. "Someone lend me a handkerchief. Someone gently wipe the tear from my eye."

Felicity was about to let him have it, but Sharrif poked her with his elbow. They would have to put up with his nasty attitude for a while. He could force them off anytime he liked.

"We're leaving the sugarcane," Grumpy said. "Which is fine. I can't stand sugarcane. There will be desert from here until Luxor. Which is not fine. I can't stand sand either."

Ramses climbed up the back of Sharrif's robe to perch upon his shoulder. A vast desert dotted with scrubby tufts of grass stretched out before them as far as he could see. To the left lay a line of green vegetation along the river. "We'll need you to look for a place to rest before long," he said to the camel.

"I don't take orders from a pussycat, especially one wearing spectacles."

Without warning, Ramses leaped from Sharrif. He landed atop the camel's head, spun around, and shimmied down his snout. "Is that so?"

The camel started to say something involving rubbish and balderdash, but he changed his mind. He was many times larger than the cat, but something in the little feline's voice gave him pause.

"Thought so," Ramses said. "Right, then. We'll stay in sight of the river until a little before sunrise. After a snooze, we'll set out into the desert. It's a more direct line to Luxor and you'll make better time. Think you can do that?"

The camel sneered and rolled his eyes, which was his way of saying, "Of course, I can."

"I think you can too," Ramses said and he gave the camel a playful swat on the nose before scampering back to his place on the saddle.

A little before sunrise, the grumpy camel approached a stand of palms upon a cool green hillock beside the Nile. "What say you, cat? Will this do for a resting place?"

"Could not have done better myself," Ramses said, and the camel shook his halter with something that might have been pleasure.

Felicity and Sharrif had not spoken for some time. Ramses suspected they had dozed off. "We'll stop here," he said, and they lifted their heads and blinked and looked around. The grumpy camel lowered them to the ground without complaint.

Ramses asked Felicity to take the reed sarcophagus out of the saddle bag. "And now go find yourselves a bed in the grass," he said. "Not too close to the river. I'll wake you in a few hours."

"What about you?" Felicity asked.

"I'm most alert at this time of night," Ramses said. "Get some rest. You too, Grumpy. And Timsah, you can sleep in the river."

The little crocodile chirped and streaked across the grass and plopped into the water.

"The rest of you, to sleep now," Ramses said. "Sweet dreams and have no fear." He crouched beside the sarcophagus with his tail flicking from side to side. "I'll be keeping watch."

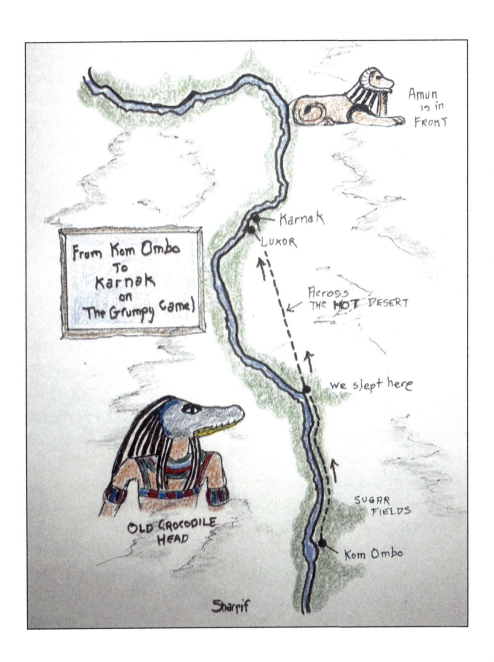

5

After Felicity and Sharrif drifted into sleep beneath the palms and the grumpy camel lay down nearby and the crocodile sank to his eyes in the shallows, Ramses ran his paw over the sarcophagus and the carved reeds. "Wherein Lies the Key to the Labyrinth of the Crocodiles," he whispered, and he pulled the lid open and gazed at the emptiness inside. "I believe our missing blue crocodile is that very key. But a key to *what*?"

The most famous labyrinth in the world was located in ancient Greece, built by Dedalus and home to the fearsome Minotaur, half bull and half man. Legends told that Dedalus got the idea after visiting an even greater labyrinth in northern Egypt. Built by Amenemhat III, it was a wondrous maze of halls and chambers so confusing that those who found their way inside had an impossibly difficult time finding their way out again.

To stumble upon a key to such a place would be a remarkable discovery. To discover the maze itself would be the find of a lifetime.

Unfortunately, it had already happened.

One of Professor Jammpot's oldest friends was an Egyptologist named Sir William Flinders Petrie*. Back in 1888, he discovered the burial chamber of Amenemhat III inside a pyramid called Hawara* in the Faiyum Oasis. When he came upon a massive slab of stone beside the pyramid, Sir William realized he had discovered the floor of the fabled Labyrinth, the only part of it that remained.

Sadly, the entire complex had been torn down in later centuries by the Romans who used the pieces to build other temples and structures.

Ramses abandoned all hope of a labyrinth. Nothing remained for the blue crocodile key to open. No lock. No door. Nothing. Only a barren, empty bedrock floor covered with a shallow layer of sand and broken bits of limestone.

Once he put the lost labyrinth out of his mind, he still had some questions. Could there be a second labyrinth? And what of the blue crocodile? It was not especially valuable. Why would the Countess von Hyss go through so much trouble to steal it? And what about the tiny writing on its belly? He wondered if Jammpot had translated any of the hieroglyphs before he disappeared.

He decided to conduct a little research when they arrived in Luxor. Until then, he had other matters to consider. He left his sleeping friends and strolled closer to the river's edge. "Timsah," he called softly. "Are you nearby?"

The crocodile emerged from under some overhanging reeds.

"You have minnows to snap up for breakfast," the cat said. "Grumpy Humpy has grass. I have whatever little squeaky thing I can find on the riverbank, but our friends won't have anything to tide them over until Luxor. How about chasing a few finny fellows up close enough for me to snag?"

Chasing, leaping and snagging, Ramses and Timsah threw themselves into the job and had a fine time of it. The baby crocodile swam deep and fast and drove the confused fish toward the shore where the cat waited to pounce.

"Bravo Tim!" he called whenever a fish appeared thrashing in the shallows and *chirp, chirp, chirp* called the crocodile when Ramses managed to catch it.

After hauling their third silvery perch ashore, little Timsah disappeared on a dive. Seconds later, Ramses noticed something floating nearby, approaching in silence, a dark figure in the river. "Uh-oh," he thought, and scooted away from the water's edge. The dark figure floated past without a sound, without a ripple. "Maybe not..."

The thing could have been a broken piece of wood, or a floating trunk from a palm tree. He watched it drift away until Timsah distracted him with another fish. But then – "no wait," Ramses thought when he saw a low ripple behind the drifting log.

It was the same ripple made by a lazy thrust of a crocodile's tail. "Awfully sly, these crocs," he thought, and he stared without moving until the ripple faded away.

Not long after, the eastern sky lightened into pale grey. "Time to get up," Ramses said, and he pawed at Felicity's cheek. He did the same to Sharrif. They stretched and yawned, and both quickly realized they were hungry and without food. Their concern turned to joy when Timsah led them to the fish lying on the riverbank.

Felicity asked Sharrif to build a fire while she cleaned the fish with the knife taken from their excavation in Kom Ombo. Within minutes, the perch were skewered on sticks and grilling over the flames. "Like fish perfume," Ramses said, sniffing the air. Felicity offered him a piece but, surprisingly, he refused. "You eat it all," he said. "You'll need it. There'll be nothing more until we reach Luxor."

The trek across the desert was long and dreary and blazing hot, with few stops along the way. Ramses never had any trouble with heat in spite of his fur. "Quite pleasant," he said while lying on his side.

"Aren't you *ever* hot?" Felicity asked after blowing the hair from her face with a puff of breath.

"Once," he replied. "Inside a volcano. Bit stuffy." He yawned. "Cold is a different beast altogether. I nearly freeze into a solid block of cat-shaped ice every time we visit London. Why do you think I attacked Aunt Ludmilla-Florence's feathered hat all those years ago?"

"You thought it was a bird."

Labyrinth of the Crocodiles

"That's what I told her, but no. I did it so Auntie would toss me out into the sleet and rain, which she did. Jammpot said it was an outrage and declared we would return to Egypt at once, as I expected he would. You begged to come with us and here we are, all thanks to a humble hop upon a hideous hat."

By day's end they passed out of the forlorn deserts and came to the city of Luxor upon the eastern bank of the Nile. Hundreds of oil lamps flickered in hundreds of windows. Cafés buzzed with voices. Smoke from hookah pipes drifted by, and Felicity and Sharrif's stomachs growled at the smells of roasting chicken and baking bread. "We can get some cool water at a well, but no dinner yet," Ramses said. "Can you hold off for a bit?"

"Carrot," said Grumpy Humpy.

"All in good time, sir," Ramses returned. "We haven't much time before the Countess closes her shop for the night." Felicity and Sharrif agreed to wait, but Grumpy Humpy said if he didn't get a carrot soon, he might become even more irritable than usual.

"If such a thing is possible," Ramses noted.

"Trust me. It is." The camel shook his halter. "Where to?"

Ramses climbed up his neck and sat atop his head. "Karnak*. I'll show you the way."

6

They passed through street upon narrow street and soon came to the enormous jumble of pillars and columns and monumental walls that formed the Temple of Karnak.

Grumpy Humpy sank to the ground with his traditional bellow and they dropped from the saddle. Ramses asked the camel to wait, and he agreed, but only after declaring the cat's simple request to be the worst thing that had ever happened to anyone – ever.

Ramses led his two friends into the ruin and to a line of sphinxes with ram heads. "The god Amun in his earthly form," he said after he hopped upon the first ram sphinx. "This one will be our meeting place if we become separated." He asked Sharrif if he could memorize a list of names, and he rattled off a list of strange Greek and Latin words that bewildered the boy. "Herodotus, *An Account of Egypt;* Manetho's *Aegyptiaca;* Strabo's *Geographica;* Volume One of Diodorus Siculus' *Bibliotheca Historia* and, finally, *Naturalis Historia* by Pliny the Elder. Got it?"

"Got it?!" Sharrif cried. "Of course, I don't got it!"

"I'll say them again."

"Impossible," Sharrif said. "They go out of my mind as soon as I hear them. I wouldn't remember one of them, never mind *all* of them."

Felicity held up her sketchpad and pencil. "Say them again."

"Herodotus*," Ramses said.

"The Greek traveler," Felicity added, writing it down.

"How do you know that?" Sharrif asked, amazed.

"We learned about him in Greek history."

Sharrif shook his head. "I don't remember that either."

Felicity tapped the pencil on the page. "No matter. You'll have this."

After Ramses listed the remaining names, he asked Sharrif to take the paper to a bookseller beside the river. "Mention my name. Tell him I'll return the books within two months. Let Timsah swim about for a bit while you're there. I expect he's dry as a stick. You can pay off Grumpy with some fat juicy carrots and put the coins in his saddlebag. Hear that, Grumpy Humpy?" Ramses called. "You've been a great help and deserve all the carrots we can find."

"Wish I could say it was a pleasure," the camel said, "but, frankly…"

Ramses ignored him. "Off you go now, Sharrif. Bring the books back here to this Amun ram sphinx. You see that building with the red awning? That's the Rose and Venom. If you arrive back here before we do, keep a close eye on it. Don't leave until we come out."

They left the shadows of the temple and said their goodbyes to Grumpy Humpy. "Tell the merchant about the coins in your saddlebag," Felicity said. "I don't think he'll be too upset you went missing."

"Who would be?" Ramses muttered behind her.

"Thank you, camel," she said, ignoring Ramses' remark. "I hope our paths cross again."

"No, you don't," said Grumpy Humpy.

"All right, I don't," Felicity admitted. "But I thank you all the same."

Sharrif grabbed the camel's stirrup and climbed onto the saddle. "On we go to carrots," he said. He tapped his heels against the camel's sides, and off they went, with the camel grumbling and claiming this to be rubbish and that to be balderdash until they were well and truly out of sight.

"Good riddance," Ramses muttered, and he turned his attention to the nearby shop with the red awning. Lantern light glowed behind the lattice-covered windows. "It won't do for us to be seen together. You shall have to go in alone."

Felicity gasped. "Alone!"

"With a new name. Ludmilla."

"Must I?"

"Everyone knows your uncle travels with his niece. Many know your name, even if they've never met you." He gazed around, looking for inspiration for a new last name. "Sandstone," he said, looking at the temple wall. "Ludmilla Sandstone, daughter of famed collector of Egyptian antiquities, Lord Sandstone."

"Lord Sandstone!" Felicity exclaimed. "But my dress! This dried mud from the Nilometer. Camel hair. And look at this lace trim. Filthy! I look nothing like a Lord's daughter."

"Days of hard travel. It explains so much."

"Can't you come with me?"

"She knows me too well," Ramses said. "Worse, Pickelhaube knows me too."

"I have no idea what I'm supposed to do."

"Distract the Countess," Ramses said. "Pickelhaube too. Keep them occupied in the front room of the shop while I snoop around the storeroom out back."

"Distract them how?" Felicity asked.

"Tell them Lord Sandstone is hoping to add to his collection of antiquities. Do not mention Amenemhat III or the Labyrinth. Don't mention anything we've discovered or talked about over the last few days."

"What *should* I mention?"

"Tell her your father is interested in a later pharaoh. Cleopatra. And finally…" Ramses hesitated so long that she poked a finger into his side. "Finally, do not be too alarmed by the Countess," he said, and he hesitated again. "She *is* rather alarming, I'm afraid."

Felicity's heart was in her throat when she approached the shop. "Rather alarming," she whispered, and wondered what Ramses meant by it.

A bell above the door clanged when she entered the Rose and Venom, but no one appeared to greet her. Lanterns cast a dull light over a collection of fake Egyptian artifacts. Most of these were plaster statues of Anubis, the jackal-headed god of embalming and death.

His black snout and pointed ears gave the Rose and Venom the somber look of a tomb.

A silver bell like the ones at a hotel desk sat on a high table near the back of the shop.

She touched it. *ding*. A beaded curtain behind the table clattered and Felicity gasped when the largest man she had ever seen came through it. Pickelhaube! He was gigantic, overwhelming, and completely unexpected; as unexpected as a water buffalo suddenly appearing from behind a delicate lace curtain. He had to bend over to avoid hitting the top of the doorframe.

He was nearly seven feet tall with a build far more like a mountain gorilla than a man. He had little piggy eyes in his great big puffy face, a blonde walrus mustache, and he wore a German military uniform and a helmet with a spike on top. An oversized billy club hung from his belt. It, too, had a spiked helmet made of iron and perfectly formed to fit over its end.

Felicity was tongue-tied. Speechless. If this brute had kidnapped Uncle Alistair there was no possible way he could escape.

"Good afternoon – evening," she stammered. "My name is Ludmilla Sandstone, sorry for my appearance, I've been traveling all day. Daughter of Lord Sandstone. In the market for..." Her mind went blank. "Is the Countess available?"

Without a word, Major Pickelhaube bent low again and retreated through the beaded curtain. Felicity grabbed the side of the table, certain she might faint. She straightened again when the monstrous Pickelhaube returned carrying a round wicker basket. Strange, Felicity thought, and she wondered if the Countess had already left for the day.

"Thandthtone," she heard someone say. "Lord Thand...."

"Stone," Felicity said, looking around the room. "Lord Sandstone."

"The name ith not familiar," the voice said.

57

Felicity looked around again but saw no one. "Countess?"

"Here."

"I don't see you," Felicity said, confused.

"My lid, Hermann-Düüfuth."

Pickelhaube lifted the top of the basket. Felicity gazed at it, puzzled. She froze with her eyes widening and spine tingling when an immense cobra rose into view, grinning hideously and flicking her tongue.

"Countess?" Felicity said, barely able to form the word.

The cobra nodded. "Counteth Therpentina von Hyth. How do you do?" She wore a single monocle over her right eye and a collar of delicate white lace that still allowed her to expand her neck hood. Being a snake, she had no hair. Even so, she wore a black hairnet that gave her a more severe look than the already severe look she was born with.

"Fine, thank you," Felicity said, finally understanding what Ramses meant by "rather alarming".

"Thplendid," the snake said with a wink behind her monocle. "I am pleathed to make your aquaintanthe."

Felicity did not see it yet, but the Countess had lost one of her fangs during a failed robbery. The accident affected her speech and made her the only snake in the known world unable to utter a proper hiss. Her *S* sounds came out as *TH*. Even so, she still managed to make everything sound like a horrible hiss even when no *S* was involved at all. She flicked her tongue. "I am thimply delighted you have dethided to thtop by and inthpect my thtore."

Felicity shuddered when she recognized the whispery voice in the tent at Kom Ombo.

What she did not realize was that someone recognized her too…or, rather, *almost* recognized her.

Major Hermann-Düüfus von Pickelhaube stared at her without blinking. Ludmilla Sandstone…he didn't recognize the name, but he had seen this girl before, he was sure of it. But when? And where?

The Countess noticed Pickelhaube's stare.

"Forgive him, my thweet angel," she said after grimacing at her servant. "Ever thinth the Great War, he cannot thpeak. His tongue was shot off, though how that happened I cannot thay." She grinned. "Come to think of it, neither can he." Felicity finally caught a glimpse of her broken fang when the Countess laughed a dry, sandy laugh. "Neither can he," the cobra repeated with a horrible snicker. "How very amuthing."

When the girl did not join in the merriment, the Countess sighed and turned to business. "Now then, my dearetht love. Ath you can thee, I have many treasureth on dithplay. Lord Thandthtone…hath he an interetht in a thpethific pharaoh?"

"Cleopatra," Felicity said. Her throat was dry.

"Ah, her," said the cobra, and Felicity shivered when the hideous Countess emerged from her basket, coil upon coil slithering out upon the table. The delicate lace around her throat made the rest of her body appear darker grey than she was, the color of a rat, or the brooding shade of a thundercloud. "Come my prethiouth waif. I am delighted to prethent to you a pritheleth relic that belonged to the magnifithent Cleopatra herthelf."

7

The Rose and Venom was a single-story building with three rooms. The shop in front was the only one open to the public. A smaller room near the front door contained only the basket the Countess used as her bedroom (Pickelhaube slept in a shed attached to the outside of the building). A third room in the back served as a garage, storage room, workshop, and was now the target of Ramses' interest.

It had a huge door (now closed and locked) and no windows but for two narrow openings near the roof, about a foot high and covered with wooden lattice. "That'll do," Ramses said, and he hopped upon a barrel and then to the top of Pickelhaube's shed and peeped inside.

A fan spiraled on the ceiling, but so slowly it did not stir the plaster dust that lay thick upon everything below. A canvas-covered motorcar took up most of the space on one end. Several large wooden crates sat on the floor beside a long table. Upon this, Ramses saw a lamp, a stack of paper, a pen, and – "there you are," he muttered when he saw the little blue crocodile.

He squeezed his head through the largest gap in the lattice. It barely fit, but no matter: if he got his head through, the rest would follow. It would not be easy to get back out, especially if he needed to make a quick getaway.

Once through, he studied the room again. A cage crowded with miserable-looking mice sat on the floor. A note pinned to the cage read: *Groceries.* Ramses shuddered. He couldn't help but feel sorry for them. "Poor chaps."

He hopped from the lattice opening to the table. The blue crocodile was the same one, no question about it. The stack of paper proved the Countess took Jammpot too. Ramses recognized his handwriting on the top page. But where was he? Had he escaped? Had she let him go after he gave them what she wanted? And what, exactly, *did* she want?

Ramses wiped his spectacles with his paw and crouched before the page filled with Jammpot's writing. *The Sacred Crocodile Sleeps in the Reeds.* That part he already knew. It was a translation of the hieroglyphs on the crocodile's back.

Further down the page...

Hail Sobek! To those who pass through the False Portal...

What was this? A translation of the much smaller belly hieroglyphs?

Ramses gently pulled at the crocodile and turned it over. "Hail Sobek. To those who pass through the False Portal," he whispered as he read the first markings. So yes. Jammpot had translated it for the snake.

He touched the crocodile again.

Before he could move it back as he found it, a loud knock came upon the garage door behind the motorcar. The beaded curtain clattered behind Ramses. His eyes shot to the lattice opening. It was too high, too narrow for a quick escape.

Swish!

The curtain parted, and with a mighty leap, Ramses sprang straight up into the air.

Major Pickelhaube lumbered into the room and strode to the garage door. He was so tall the top of his spiked helmet nearly touched the ceiling fan where Ramses crouched atop one of the slowly revolving blades.

The giant opened the garage door. Four men in robes and turbans came in. "The boat is ready," said one. Pickelhaube pointed to a crate beside the mouse cage. The men shifted the crate through the door. After watching them lift it onto a donkey cart, Pickelhaube closed the door and made his way back toward the showroom. When he passed the table, he stopped. His helmet spike was so close to the fan, Ramses could have batted it with his paw.

Pickelhaube touched the little blue crocodile, now lying on its back.

That was not how he left it.

He looked around the room.

He checked behind the remaining crates. He inspected the shelves on the wall. He gazed at the lattice window and peered under the table. He looked everywhere but straight up where Ramses spun around and around, only inches from his head.

Satisfied, he started to leave…but stopped again. He stepped up to the table and moved the lamp. Ramses' whiskers drooped at the sight of one of his pawprints on the table, clearly visible in the plaster dust.

The massive army officer straightened and moved the lamp back. Had he seen the pawprint? Ramses could not tell. The giant picked up the blue crocodile and dropped it into his pocket. He did the same with Jammpot's translation. With no further look around, he left the storeroom. The beaded curtain clattered behind him.

Ramses had to act fast. He leaped from the fan to the lattice opening. As expected, he had much more difficulty getting back out than he had getting in. Once through, he dropped down upon the shed roof and he shot across the street into the Temple of Karnak.

"Sharrif!"

"Here." The boy rose from behind their ram-headed sphinx. "I have the books."

"Well done," Ramses said, and he asked him if he had seen four men and a crate.

"They left the shop a few minutes ago. They had a donkey cart."

"Follow them," Ramses said. "They're heading for the dock, which means they are heading for a boat. Timsah…" The little crocodile poked his snout out of the boy's robe. "Sharrif is going to put you in the river. Keep an eye on that crate. If they load it onto a boat, keep an eye on that too."

chirp.

"Good show," Ramses said. "Wait for us at the docks," he said to Sharrif. "Leave the books here. Go now, both of you. Follow that donkey cart. There's not a moment to lose!'"

8

After Sharrif limped down the darkened street with Timsah in his arms, Ramses squeezed back through the lattice opening into the storeroom. Without a sound, he dropped to the table where he stared at his pawprint in the dust. How *could* he have been so careless?

He dropped down beside the mouse cage. Thirty or so miserable mice huddled inside. "Evening, friends." They shivered in fear. Their little whiskers quivered. "Yes, I'm a cat - quite obvious, really, but let that go for now. You are in a bit of a pickle. Truth is, you are in an entire briny barrel of pickles. Why is that?" Ramses mouthed the word "snake" and the mice shuddered. "Trusting me will not be easy," he said, "but desperate times call for desperate measures, and I may very well be your last desperate hope. What say you?"

The mice did not move. They did not say a word.

"Be brave little mice," Ramses said gently. "Last desperate hopes do not always come along. When one does, you must snap it up as you might a crumb of cheese."

One of the trembling rodents stepped forward. "I'm in," he squeaked.

"What's your name?" Ramses asked the first little mouse.

"Omar."

"I need your help, Omar."

"And you've got it," the mouse said with a determined gleam in his eye. "Tell us what to do."

Inside the Rose and Venom, the Countess slithered over a countertop to a display case filled with items made of cheap worthless tin covered with gold paint and gemstones made of glass. "You'll note the necklath with the thapphire in the thenter." She flicked her tongue at an obviously fake gemstone in a necklace made of brass.

"Can you read hieroglyphth, my dear?"

"Yes," Felicity said. "I'm still learning, but I can read them fairly well."

"I, alath, cannot. Never thaw the need. You thee the tiny thymbolth upon the gemthtone? I'm told they read, 'Thith belongth to Cleopatra. Don't touch.' And there you have it. That magnifithent trinket hung around the thlender neck of Cleopatra herthelf. I have the paperth to prove it. Do you know how she died?"

"Suicide," Felicity said.

"Thuithide, yeth. But how?"

"She ordered her servants to hide a snake in a basket of figs," Felicity said. "An asp*. When they brought the basket to her, she reached inside and let the asp bite her."

"And do you know another name for an athp?" the Countess asked with a wide grin. Before Felicity could answer, the serpent exclaimed with delight: "Cobra!"

"I didn't know."

"Now you do. Oh, what a gloriouth epithode. Took up three entire chapterth in *The Book of Cobra*. And how very proud I am of the fact that Cleopatra died of a venomouth bite from my very own great-great-great-great-great-great…"

As there were 14,362 "greats" to get through before she would reach the word grandmother, Pickelhaube had plenty of time to think about the pawprint on the storeroom table. It could have been made by any stray cat, but the possibility that it was the mark of the hideous Ramses Faro made him suspicious. Faro was a well-known friend and partner of Professor Alistair Jammpot. This thought led to the enjoyable memory of Jammpot struggling but unable to escape his powerful grip, and suddenly - Ah! Another memory!

He *had* seen this girl before.

Back at Kom Ombo. He had opened the flap of Jammpot's tent. This girl now studying the fake necklaces was the one he saw leaving the campsite with a coil of rope over her shoulder. Her name was not Ludmilla Sandstone. It was Felicity Jammpot! How did she get out of that well? He thought for certain he had taken care of her when he cut the rope.

He now had no doubt about whose pawprint lay upon the table in the storeroom.

He dashed off a quick note upon a notepad. Soon after the Countess had passed the 87th "great" in her list of ancestors, he tapped his massive hand upon the desk bell.

ding.

"Now what?" the Countess asked, irritated by the interruption. He plodded across the shop and dropped the note upon the display case. The cobra stared at it.

Felicity looked at it too, but the message was in German. She couldn't read it, but it made her anxious. The way the Major stared at her did the same. "Is everything all right?"

The cobra stared at her too, without expression, and then, suddenly, "Forgive him, my child," she said with a ghastly smile. "I promithed Major Pickelhaube we would go to hith favorite rethtaurant for tea and honey cake. Café Happy Baboon. Perfectly thcrumptiouth." She blinked at the Major. "Be patient, Hermann-Düüfuth. We shall end thith very thoon." Turning back, she whispered, "Come clother, my thweet child. Marvel at the jewelth, how they thparkle in the light."

Felicity bent down for a closer look.

A ripple ran down the length of the serpent. She edged toward her, closer by an inch…and then another. "Do you know *The Book of Cobra?*" the Countess asked.

Without looking at her, Felicity said she had never heard of it. She sensed the sinewy snake moving closer the way we sense someone is staring at us even when our back is turned.

"An anthient book," the Countess murmured. "Filled with legendth of every legendary cobra who thlithered through the land of Egypt. One tale has fathinated me all my life, a tale from the time of Pharaoh Amenemhat III."

Felicity froze. "Amenemhat?" she repeated, breathless.

"And a robbery in Kom Ombo two thouthand yearth ago," the Countess continued. "Do you know of Kom Ombo?"

Felicity tried to shake her head, but she couldn't get it to move.

The cobra coiled upon the display case, only inches away. "*The Book of Cobra* recordth what the cobrath of old found there. A key to a fabulouth treasure in an equally fabluouth labyrinth."

"Key…" Felicity whispered. She could say nothing more. She felt a light flick upon her arm, as soft as a fly landing. She closed her eyes when she realized the serpent's tongue had brushed against her.

"A key in the form of a thacred blue crocodile."

Felicity's voice shuddered when she told her she didn't know a thing about it.

The Countess reared up, poised and tense. "Oh, but you do," she said. "You and that infernal cat Ramtheeth Faro!"

Felicity's eyes shot to the Countess and she gasped to see her lace collar suddenly part and her cobra's hood spread out with a snap. Her mouth gaped wide. Her single fang glistened.

Before she could strike, and before Felicity could scream, there came a strangled cry from Major Pickelhaube behind them. He shuddered with disgust when a mouse squirmed up from his collar and climbed onto his mustache. Four more squiggled out of his sleeves. He spun around, and Felicity goggled at a swarm of mice scampering over his back.

The Countess wailed in dismay: "My grotherieth!"

The beaded curtain clattered, and Felicity's heart leaped when Ramses Faro shot through the air like a cannonball and landed in a crouch upon the countertop. "Evening Countess," he said. Before the startled cobra could react, Ramses said, "The door, Felicity. Go!"

She dashed to the front door. The bell clanged when she opened it. Pickelhaube shot forward. He grabbed her by the arm and dragged her back into the shop.

The mice leaped and sprang and scattered from the Major like grey popcorn from an open pan. They bounded through the door and into the safety of the night, every one of them squeaking: "Free! Free! We're free!"

Omar was the last to go. He spun around on the threshold: "Hey snake!"

When she turned, he spun around again and wiggled his little mouse behind at her. "The *idea!*" the Countess sputtered in shock. With a whoop of glee, the cheeky little mouse saluted Ramses, thumbed his nose at the cobra, and dashed off after his friends.

The Countess recovered at once. "Pin her down!" she shouted at Pickelhaube. The giant tossed Felicity to the floor. He set his heavy boot down upon her chest, and from behind him came a surprisingly calm voice, "Oh, I rather think not," immediately followed by a yowling, slashing, ball of fur. Slash! Slash! Slash!

Pickelhaube fell back. Felicity rolled from under his boot. "Go!" Ramses called. Felicity leaped to her feet and dashed through the door at the same time Ramses leaped from the giant onto the jewelry case.

"You!" the Countess said with a deadly glare.

"Me!" Ramses returned with a smirk.

"I shall bite and thrike and thend my venom into your veinth."

"Ooooo, scary canary," Ramses said with another smirk.

"Don't you thcary canary me, you intholent rathcal!" the furious Countess shouted.

67

The insolent rascal hopped atop a statue where he crouched between Anubis' ears, which made the jackal-god look like he had chosen to wear a fur hat in the underworld. "I don't know what you've done with Jammpot, but know this," he said. "I *will* find him. And if any harm has come to him…" He held up his right paw. Five claws slowly emerged from his paw fur and shimmered in the light.

"I thuppothe you think I am imprethed with thothe thilly little clawth," the Countess said. With shocking speed, she raced over the counter with her mouth gaping wide. Ramses sprang away and she collided with the statue's ear. Her monocle shot from her eye and clacked against the wall.

Ramses streaked toward the door, but Pickelhaube slammed it before he could slip through. "Catch him!" the cobra shouted. "Thtrike him!"

Ramses sprang onto another counter and bounced from statue to statue to statue. Major Pickelhaube pulled his iron-helmeted club from his belt. Ramses spun around and raised his paw again. "This will not end well, Pickelpuss."

Pickelhaube glared at the cat, fuming at the nickname.

"Pay no attention!" the cobra shouted. "Bring that horrid mammal to me!"

Pickelhaube strode toward him, chest expanded and eyes ablaze. He brought his club down upon the statue and shattered it to pieces, but as always, Ramses was too fast.

He sprang onto Pickelhaube's sleeve. Out came the claws. "Told you," he said, and he gave him a quick jab before he jumped to the floor. Pickelhaube touched his nose, looked at his fingers, saw the blood – and Ramses shot through the beaded curtain.

Into the storeroom he went, onto the table, and he sailed into the air.

He judged his target in a split second and stretched until he looked more like an arrow than a cat, and *whoosh!*

Straight through the hole in the lattice without grazing a single whisker.

He overshot the shed and landed on all four feet in the road.

Seconds later he caught up with Felicity and together they dashed into the Temple of Karnak while the hiss that wasn't a hiss called into the night. "I'll not forget thith, Ramtheeth Faro. You will not ethcape! I shall hunt you down and catch you. And when I do...I shall thwallow you whole!"

III.

VOYAGE OF THE WIND CAT

Ramses Faro

1

When Ramses caught up with Felicity in the Temple of Karnak and discovered she had not been injured by Pickelhaube, he rubbed his face against hers and purred and purred and purred. "I'm fine," she said with a laugh, but he would not stop. "I thought you were hurt – *purr, purr* – the way that oaf Pickelhaube – *purr, purr, purr* – tossed you to the floor."

"What an awful thing he is," she exclaimed. "And *her!*"

Ramses stopped purring. "Rather alarming?" he asked, and Felicity wholeheartedly agreed.

They heard a door whine open and an engine roar to life. Ramses climbed onto Felicity's shoulder and they watched the black motorcar pull out of the Rose and Venom with Pickelhaube at the wheel, holding a bloody handkerchief over his nose, and the Countess in the back seat, with her small head covered by a veil made of black lace.

"They have the sacred blue crocodile," Ramses said. "I saw Pickelhaube put it in his pocket."

"And Uncle Alistair?"

"They have him too. I'm sure of it. They're going to the riverside docks, I'm sure of that too. I sent Sharrif on ahead."

Felicity dropped the small books Sharrif brought from the bookseller into the reed sarcophagus, tucked it under her arm, and off they went. By the time they arrived at the river, the motorcar sat empty and still beside a loading dock. Ramses assumed the Countess had gone aboard one of the boats – but which one?

The east bank of the Nile at Luxor was jam-packed with riverboats of every kind: steamboats, fishing boats, luxury sailing yachts called dahabeeyahs *, and a fleet of the smaller felucca sailboats that clustered along the muddy bank.

Sharrif beckoned to Ramses and Felicity from behind a mound of cotton bales. "I can't tell which boat is theirs," he said. He pointed to a group of men standing guard at the black car. "I didn't dare let them see me, so I put Timsah in the river to spy for us."

"Well done," Ramses said, and he hopped onto a cotton bale and looked from one end of the waterfront to the other. "The Countess told Felicity about a cake shop called the Café Happy Baboon. You two go there now. Your stomachs have been growling like wild beasts since sunset."

"And you?" Felicity asked.

"Slinking and skulking, as always," Ramses returned. "Timsah may need some help."

An engine started. Felicity peeped around the bale. "The car," she said. "One of the guards is driving. He's alone. Maybe taking it back to the shop?"

"Which means the Countess and Pickelhaube plan to sail upon the river," Ramses said. "You go now. I'll come for you after little leathery friend and I discover how they plan to do it."

After Felicity and Sharrif eagerly trudged off to the Café Happy Baboon, Ramses hopped off the cotton bale for a riverside prowl.

He did not bother to inspect the smaller feluccas. The Countess would need a boat large enough to carry that mysterious wooden crate. "With Jammpot inside," Ramses thought. He had no reason to think it. He did not see Jammpot put into the crate. He did not hear pounding from inside, or a muffled voice. He *felt* it.

Ramses and Professor Alistair Jammpot had been particular friends since the day the professor came upon an abandoned kitten beside the Great Sphinx near Cairo. All alone, swarming with fleas, one eye crusted over, and with a nasty cough, he told him his name. "Faro. Ramses Faro."

"And mine is Alistair Jammpot," said the professor, doffing his wide-brimmed straw hat. "How do you do?" The kitten coughed and wheezed. Jammpot crouched and held out his hand and Ramses crept onto his palm. Lifting him up to his face, the professor said, "Now see here. I have no interest in acquiring a pet." The kitten's ears drooped. "What I mean is…that is to say," he stammered, afraid he had hurt the kitten's feelings. "I don't care much for the word 'pet.' I much prefer the word 'friend'. Does that appeal to you?" The kitten nodded. "Now that we've cleared that up, might you care to join me in my travels? Before you answer, you should know that I tend to get into a bit of a pickle now and then. Still appeal to you?"

Ramses was not very strong in those days, but with his last ounce of energy, he sprang from the professor's palm onto his collar and rubbed his cheek against his jaw and purred the loudest purr he had ever purred up to that point in his young life.

The bond they forged that day was unbreakable.

They often did not need to talk for they knew what the other was thinking. Ramses knew when Jammpot was approaching, even when he could not see or hear him. He knew — he *knew*! – the professor had not escaped from the Countess and Pickelhaube, and he knew it the moment he saw the crate taken from the storeroom. The Countess had imprisoned him as surely as she had imprisoned Omar the mouse and his chums. "And I shall release you the same way," Ramses said.

He left the cluster of feluccas and approached the larger dahabeeyahs. He climbed aboard the first like a tightrope walker, balancing on a line from the dock to the deck. Nearly all were deserted, though a few had dim lights and soft voices within.

He jumped from one to another and heard a small splash below. "Good show," he whispered when he saw Timsah's eyes emerge from the water. "Do you know which boat?"

chirp

"Carry on."

From boat to boat he hopped and sprang as Timsah led him through the maze of masts and ropes and decks. Eventually the crocodile swam up close to the largest and most luxurious dahabeeyah of all. Armed guards patrolled the decks, one in the bow and two in the stern.

The long barge-like vessel had two massive sails, now furled upon the booms attached to the masts. An open-air drawing room covered by an awning served as an upper deck. Ramses saw a name painted on the bow in Arabic, German, and English, and if nothing before told him this boat belonged to the Countess, its name certainly did.

The Tasty Rat

He crept as close as he dared upon a neighboring boat and swiveled his large ears, listening….and hearing….

…a fisherman's campfire crackling on the shore.

...a night bird upon the west riverbank, another Egyptian nightjar with its call of *toc toc toc churrrrr!*

....a hum of voices from a nearby coffee house or café.

....and *"yes, yes, there it is"* he thought.

From inside the boat, low and breathy, a hiss that wasn't a hiss.

2

Café Happy Baboon was a favorite gathering place of apes and monkeys from all levels of society. On that night it was nearly full. Felicity and Sharrif found a corner table near the kitchen – it was not the best, but it was the only one not occupied by furry grey baboons.

Overall, they were a civilized bunch. Many of the baboon gentlemen wore straw hats or turbans. Some wore ties. The lady baboons wore hats adorned with ribbons and fruit (mostly bananas that would end up missing before the night was through). A huge slouching baboon with the fur on his head parted in the middle and wearing a greasy apron shuffled up to their table and handed each of them a menu. "Tea?"

"Yes, please," Felicity said.

The baboon snapped his fingers. "Nicky! Tea."

A spry little monkey dashed over with glasses of steaming mint tea balanced on a tray.

"Thank you, Nicky," Felicity said, and the monkey grinned and bowed and hopped away.

The baboon waiter wiped his nose with the back of his paw. "What'll you have?"

A lady baboon wearing a hat loaded with grapes leaned from her chair beside Felicity. "Might I recommend the fig tart with pistachios?" she said with a wink. "Heavenly."

"I'll have that," Felicity told the waiter. "And honey cakes."

Sharrif squinted at the menu. "Do you have roast chicken?"

The hubbub around them ceased at once. All the baboons lowered their spoons and turned to stare at him.

The waiter glared. He tapped his paw on Sharrif's menu. "Can't you read?"

Sharrif flushed. His face turned red.

Felicity jumped in at once. "Of course, he can read. He asked a question, that's all."

"I see," the waiter said, clearly believing the question was not a very bright one.

"It's a monkey café," Felicity whispered over the table. "They don't serve meat."

"We serve grasshoppers now and then, but only on holidays," the waiter said with an impatient sigh. "And today is not a holiday so don't ask for grasshoppers."

Sharrif nodded with a smile and an apologetic shrug. "I haven't been to many cafes."

"Obviously," the waiter said. "So what'll you have?"

Sharrif was nervous. He didn't know what to say. He felt rushed by the waiter, who stood beside him and tapped his pad with his pencil and muttered, "Again, no grasshoppers, so don't ask."

Sharrif closed his menu with a snap. "I'll have the same thing she's having."

In the end, they decided on the fig tart with pistachios, a bowl of nut-stuffed dates, rice pudding, vanilla ice cream, and Felicity's favorite, a cake soaked in honey called *basbousa**.

They had not eaten a thing since the fish breakfast way back near Kom Ombo and they happily attacked the desserts. Honey dribbled down their chins. Powdered sugar clung to the ends of their noses. Whipped cream stuck to their sleeves, and truly, it was one of the best (and sweetest) dinners they could remember.

A band of monkeys strolled onto a small stage at the back of the café. "The singer's name is Abdullah Valentino," the grape-hatted baboon whispered to Felicity. "My favorite singing ape of all time, makes my heart go pitty-pat."

The monkey band took their places, and then came Abdullah the Ape in black tie and tails with his fur slicked back with grease. He specialized in romantic ape songs such as *Swinging on the Vines of My Heart* and *I Groom You by Moonlight,* and the patrons of the Café Happy Baboon sighed with delight.

Right in the middle of Abdullah's passionate *When You Screech at Me,* Felicity let out a startled cry when Ramses suddenly appeared on their table, upsetting the teacups, and overturning a pile of pastries. "Terribly sorry," the cat said.

"I *do* wish you would look before you leap." Felicity sopped up the tea with a napkin. "No need to do this every time."

"I don't do it *every* time," Ramses said, though he admitted he did upset the table every second or third time. "Have you had your fill? If not, we shall take it with us."

"Why?" Sharrif asked. He was enjoying the music and the tea and was not nearly ready to give up the honey cakes and cream.

"I found her boat," Ramses returned. "They're setting sail."

Back behind the bales of cotton, they watched *The Tasty Rat* cast off her lines and drift into the deeper part of the river.

"They hope to get away from us," Ramses said. "To which I say no." He turned to Sharrif. "We need a boat."

Sharrif studied the row of feluccas lining the shore and pointed to one that (to Felicity and Ramses) looked exactly like all the others. "That one," he said. "Don't worry. We'll pay for it."

"How will we find the owner?" Felicity asked.

"I'll show you," Sharrif replied. "First, take most of the money out of your purse." After Felicity did as he asked, they found a lantern and lit it. "Don't slink and skulk," Sharrif instructed. "We want them to see us." After they climbed aboard, he untied the boat from the dock. "Go sit in the stern."

"Where?" Felicity asked, looking around.

"The back of the boat," Sharrif said. "The front is called the bow. Swing the lantern back and forth."

Moments later, they heard voices shouting from the street. A gang of fishermen dashed toward them. Sharrif shoved the boat from the dock and hopped onto the bow. "Who owns this boat?" he called to the men in Arabic.

"I do!" said a tall, broad-shouldered man. "Bring it back!"

Sharrif lifted the purse and shook it. "I'll double it when I come back in…." He looked at Ramses.

"One month," the cat said.

"In one month!" He threw the purse, and the man caught it. "It's more than you'll make in three months as a fisherman," Sharrif said.

The boat's owner opened the purse and tipped the coins into palm. "Many thanks to you," he called to his departing boat. "May God go with you!"

"And with you, good sir!" Sharrif returned.

He guided the boat toward the middle of the river. "I'll need help to row."

"Help from me?" Felicity asked. She looked up at the mast. "I wouldn't know where to begin."

"I'll teach you. Ramses, are you strong enough to hold the tiller?"

"Strong enough!" Ramses repeated. "Me? My dear boy, of course I'm strong enough to hold a tiller," he insisted, and he shook his head and bristled his whiskers before asking, "What's a tiller?"

"That wooden handle in the stern," Sharrif said. "It steers the boat, the same as a wheel in a bigger boat. Put your front paws on the handle. Try to keep it steady. Where's Timsah?" They heard a chirp from the river. Sharrif leaned over and scooped him up into the boat. "You help Ramses steer."

Sharrif set him down on the seat beside Ramses, and together the cat and the crocodile set their front paws on the wooden handle and did their best to keep it from moving. Ramses looked at Timsah and winked. "I'm as surprised as you are."

"There isn't enough wind for the sails," Sharrif said. "The Countess' dahabeeyah will drift with the current. We'll keep up with it, but not too close. Is that clear?" he asked, and Felicity smiled and saluted him.

"Aye-aye Captain!"

3

In the stateroom aboard *The Tasty Rat*, Major Hermann-Düüfus von Pickelhaube pried the lid off the wooden crate and hauled Alistair Jammpot into the lamplight. "Could have done with a few more air holes in this thing," the professor said, gasping and blinking. "Frightfully stuffy, if you ask me."

"Which no one did," said the Countess. She lay coiled upon a chaise lounge with her hairnet, monocle, and lace collar in place, prim and proper and perfectly at ease aboard her luxurious vessel. "You should conthider yourthelf fortunate I did not leave you in there to thuffocate."

Uncle Alistair started to say something but thought better of it. Instead, he resorted to the thing he always did when facing a difficult situation. "What are the chances of a cup of tea?"

The cobra nodded toward a guard at the cabin door.

Ramses Faro

"Black tea, if you please, milk on the side," Uncle Alistair called as the guard departed. "And do make it piping hot, won't you?" He noted the round porthole windows and felt the mild rocking of the floor. "Are we on a boat?"

The Countess nodded. "My private dahabeeyah. We are thailing north."

"North!" He started to climb out of the crate but Pickelhaube stopped him with his club. "Oh, do put that away. I can't very well conduct a conversation from the interior of a crate."

Pickelhaube looked at the Countess. She nodded and he lowered the club.

Uncle Alistair climbed out. He straightened his jacket, smoothed his silky mustache, and pushed his black hair out of his eyes. "How far north?"

"Quite far. To the Land of the Thacred Crocodileth."

"The Faiyum Oasis? Oh, surely not," Uncle Alistair said with a frown. The Countess did not respond. "We *are* going there," he continued. "I can tell by your unpleasant stare. You have no need to take me with you. I told you everything I know, which is essentially nothing. I translated that little blue chap for you, front and back. My niece Felicity is still at camp at Kom Ombo. I should like very much to check up on her."

"Only your nieth Felithity?" the Countess asked.

"Our friend Sharrif Aziz is with her."

"And what about a thertain cat?"

"Cat?" he repeated, casually. "By which you mean....?"

"By which I mean *cat*!" the Countess shouted. "Fur, four pawth, tail, whithkers." She glanced at Pickelhaube's nose. "Horrid little prickly clawth."

"Oh, *that* sort of cat," said Uncle Alistair. "You must mean Ramses Faro. Haven't seen him in ages, disagreement over a tin of sardines, you know how those things are, snowballed out of control."

Labyrinth of the Crocodiles

He looked at Pickelhaube and also noticed the scratches on his nose. Ramses' work, no question about it. He hid his smile by covering his mouth with his hand as if about to cough.

"Shameleth liar," the cobra said. "We know you were with him."

Uncle Alistair smiled openly. No sense in hiding it if they already knew. He turned to the silent giant beside the crate. "Oh, I say, whatever happened to your proboscis? Close shave?"

Pickelhaube scowled. The cobra nodded toward a chair opposite her chaise lounge. "Have a theat, Alithtair. I've had a cabin made up for you. You will thtay with me for a time."

Uncle Alistair sat in the chair and the guard brought in a tray of tea and biscuits. "Cheers, mate," he said to the guard, and he dipped his biscuit into his tea and settled back in his chair. "Now then. The Faiyum Oasis. Why?"

"Becauthe of that," the Countess said and nodded at the little blue crocodile on a nearby table. "The key to the Labyrinth."

Uncle Alistair snorted. "I told you back in Kom Ombo, there is no labyrinth. There hasn't been a labyrinth in two thousand years. It's unlikely that little blue chap is the key to anything." Uncle Alistair dipped his biscuit again. "Speaking of unlikely...I've often wondered, how is it that a common, though unusually large, Egyptian cobra has inherited a title usually reserved for German nobility? Certainly not by birth. You were born in Egypt, I assume."

"In the Thahara."

"Where you should have stayed," said Uncle Alistair. "You'd have caused a lot less trouble there. So you didn't acquire your title by birth, and you certainly didn't acquire it by marriage. After all, who would marry a thing like you? Good heavens. Absurd on the face of it."

"You theem to doubt I am a true Counteth."

"Seem to doubt it? No, Countess. I *do* doubt it. With every fiber of my being. But let us assume you truly are a Countess from the land of strudel and sauerkraut. How could such an unexpected thing have happened?"

The Countess leaned back against the chaise with her neck dropping into an elegant S shape. "One thummer morning, in the thpringtime of my youth, I accthidentally crept into the luggage of a handthome nobleman who had come to Egypt on holiday. Count Frederick Heinrich Schnitzel von Hyth. He took me home with him. By mithtake. We thailed to the port of Bremerhaven, and from there went by rail to Berlin with me in his thteamer trunk – a reluctant thtow-away."

"And this Count Frederick Heinrich Schnitzel von Hyss, he…I suppose he…what? Adopted you?"

"He would have. I am thertain he would have, but he never had the chanth. When he opened the thteamer trunk – you can imagine my thurprithe, Alithtair, to thuddenly find mythelf in a thrange new world. Due to the unexthpected nature of it all, I…." She cleared her throat and lowered her eyes, as if trying to avoid Uncle Alistair's gaze. "I did not mean to do it."

"You don't mean to say you bit him?" Uncle Alistair asked with one eyebrow raised,

She sniffed and turned away, biting her lower lip.

Uncle Alistair stared. "Did you really?" He snapped off half his biscuit. "That is – did you *really*?" He crunched as he chewed. "You bit the Count?"

"He thtartled me."

"But, but, but that means…are you telling me you poisoned him?"

"Accthident."

"The very man you claim would have adopted you had you not unexpectedly popped out of his steamer trunk and sunk your fangs into an artery?"

"A regrettable error."

"But that's not how inheritance happens," Uncle Alistair exclaimed. "One cannot simply dose a chap with venom and expect his titles and property to come your way. It isn't done."

The cobra swayed and glared. "I inherited everything," she insisted. "Title, property, a cathle along the Rhine, a country ethtate in the Black Foretht…I even inherited hith manthervant, Major Hermann-Düüfuth von Pickelhaube." When Uncle Alistair began to object, she said in a firm, stiff voice: "Think what you will, but the fact remainth, I *am* The Counteth Therpentina von Hyth."

"Oh, you are not, you perfectly ridiculous serpent. You are no more a Countess than I am a snake charmer." He paused. "Have I charmed you?"

"Thertainly not."

"There. You see? And as for the Labyrinth…there is nothing left. Not a stone, not a pillar, not a brick."

"Tho you thay," said the snake. "According to the *Book of Cobra*…"

"Whatever beastly thing *that* is."

She started again, in a louder, firm voice. "According to the Labyrinth of the Crocodileth ith real. The treasure of the crocodileth ith real too."

"If that is so, then the *Book of Cobra* is as perfectly ridiculous as you are," said Uncle Alistair. "The Labyrinth was completely destroyed. The Romans tore it all down. You know how they are. This entire expedition is a colossal waste of time."

The Countess relaxed upon her chaise lounge. "We shall thee," she said. "In the meantime, you are free to wander the boat. But beware, Alithtair. You will be watched, day and night." To Pickelhaube she said, "Put a guard outthide his cabin door. They are to

85

follow him on deck. Tell them to never let him out of thight. Tell them, ethpecially, to keep an eye out for any thign of that thneaky cat."

4

The following morning dawned blue and clear and sun-drenched, with a warm breeze blowing off the western desert to make for a glorious day upon the river. Sharrif taught Felicity how to raise the sails. "I'll take the tiller," he said to Ramses, and he turned the boat this way and that until the breeze puffed out the sail in a billowing cloud of white.

"Bravo Sharrif!" Felicity cried and Ramses leaped into her lap and turned to face the bow with the wind in his whiskers and a purr in his throat.

Timsah wanted to swim alongside, but Sharrif told him they were going too fast. "I'll let the sail down a bit later and you can swim all you like. Come. Sit on my lap. Help me steer the...hmmm. What's the name of this boat?"

Felicity set Ramses down and leaned over the back of the boat. "It's in Arabic. Can't quite...I think one word is *wind*."

Sharrif leaned back and read it. "Perfect!" he said, and he pointed at Ramses. "Named in honor of our leader. *Wind Cat*."

Ramses stretched his back into an upside-down U. "A splendid name."

On the way back to the bow, Felicity pulled the small books out of the reed sarcophagus and read the cover of the first. "*An Account of Egypt*."

"Written over two thousand years ago," Ramses said as he snuck back onto her lap.

"Why did you want it?" she asked.

"Some of these ancients saw the Labyrinth with their own eyes. I am hoping they've left a clue of some kind, something to tell us what the sacred crocodile might mean." He crawled off her lap again. "Why don't you take the *Account of Egypt*. I'll take this one." Ramses adjusted his spectacles and squinted. "By a Roman chap named Strabo." He opened the book with his paw. "And Sharrif, you can take…"

Sharrif spoke right up. "That's all right. I'm fine sailing the boat."

They spent the following two days in sunny splendor, with Ramses and Felicity deep in study and Sharrif making sure they had a smooth and fast sail — but not too fast, as he tried always to stay out of sight of *The Tasty Rat*. It was all so carefree and lovely, and it might have been a completely happy voyage, but for the dark cloud of worry about Uncle Alistair.

Ramses tapped Felicity's book with his paw. "Any luck?"

"A little," she said. "Listen to this."

Ramses called back to Sharrif. "You listen too. You may hear something or think of something we will not."

"I doubt it," Sharrif muttered to himself. He shrugged and adjusted one of the lines and studied the water up ahead.

Felicity turned onto her stomach and leaned on her elbows with the book in front and read aloud: "*I saw this labyrinth myself and it is a wonder even greater than the pyramids. It has twelve courts, and there are double sets of chambers, and their number is three thousand.*"

"Three thousand chambers?" Sharrif asked. "Is such a thing possible?"

"So he says. Fifteen hundred on the upper level and fifteen hundred on the lower."

Sharrif whistled and shook his head. "No wonder everyone got lost."

Felicity agreed and returned to the book. "*Of the underground chambers I was only told. The Egyptian priests would by no means show them, these being the burial tombs of the kings who built this labyrinth, and of the sacred crocodiles.*"

"The Sacred Crocodiles," Ramses repeated. "Read on, if you please."

Felicity nodded. "*The passages through the rooms caused us countless confusion. At the corner where the labyrinth ends, there stands a pyramid. The road to this pyramid is made underground.*"

"Why would they make an underground road," Sharrif asked from the tiller, but no one had an answer. Felicity closed her book. "That was all I could find," she said. "What do you have?"

Ramses opened his book and pushed up his glasses. Using his paws, he flipped the pages until he reached one in the middle. "*Inside the great labyrinth are chambers, which are numerous and have winding passages. The priests there hold in very great honor the crocodile called the Petsuchos*, the Son of Sobek…*"

"Sobek?" Sharrif interjected. "Isn't that Old Crocodile-head?"

"The Nile river god," Ramses said. "And this sacred crocodile is called the *Petsuchos*, The Son of Sobek, '*which is fed by the priests, and is offered jewels and gold and is tame to the priests.*' That's all I found in this one."

He opened a second book and told them it described the same bewildering maze of halls and chambers. The labyrinth was filled with columns of stone, he told them, and statues of gods and kings, and when someone passed through the gateway, there came a terrifying rumble of thunder. "*Also,*" Ramses read, "*most of the labyrinth must be travelled in darkness.*"

"Sounds awful," Felicity said.

"Sounds *really* awful," Sharrif agreed. "I'm glad they tore it all down."

"I'm not," Ramses said, closing the book. "I should have loved to visit such a place."

"Oh no!" Sharrif suddenly cried and he reached for a line. "Hold on!" The felucca's boom swung and sent the boat over so far that the water washed up onto the deck.

"What happened?" Felicity asked.

"*The Tasty Rat*," Sharrif said. "It's right ahead of us, on the other side of that little island. They must have stopped early for the night."

Ramses dashed to the stern and stood beside Sharrif. "Did they see us?"

Sharrif shrugged. "I got out of sight as fast as I could, but I don't know."

"Can you take us closer to that island?" Ramses asked.

Sharrif did as he asked and dropped the stone tied to a rope that they used as an anchor. "Now what?"

Without answering, Ramses leaped onto the mast. He dug his claws in and scooted up to perch with all four feet on the very top. From there, he saw *The Tasty Rat* over the trees. "And there you are," he whispered at the sight of Uncle Alistair strolling on the deck with his hands clasped behind his back. A second man appeared behind him carrying a rifle.

He shimmied down again.

"Think they saw us?" Sharrif asked.

"We can't be certain," Ramses said. "I hoped to put this off until we chose the proper time. But chance has chosen for us."

"Which means what?" Felicity asked.

"Which means we're going to rescue your uncle."

"When?"

"Tonight."

5

Ramses paced the deck as the sun dropped but said nothing more. Felicity and Sharrif sat in the stern with the tiller between them. "Do you think he has a plan?" Sharrif whispered.

"If he doesn't have one now, he soon will," Felicity returned, also in a whisper.

"Have any of his plans not worked?"

"A few," she admitted.

"What happens then?"

"He comes up with a new one."

"And do the new plans work?" Sharrif asked.

Felicity looked at the cat sitting on the bow with his ridiculously large ears straight up and his tail twitching from side to side. "Always."

Ramses stretched and strolled to the back of the boat. "Is Timsah in the river?"

chirp

"I'll need you for this," Ramses called over the side. Sharrif lifted him out of the water and set him on the deck, and they sat in the fading sunlight, gazing at the cat, waiting. "We must not light the lantern from here on," Ramses began. "No fire, no light of any kind. This is what we'll do."

He told them of his plan, involving the island, the river, a good deal of slinking and skulking, and some of the secret signals they had developed over time. On this night, they decided on a birdcall (the call of the Egyptian nightjar), and a tap on the side of the nose. "Is all that clear?" he asked when finished.

"Clear," said Felicity, and "Clear," said Sharrif, and completely unexpected, they heard a soft, high, chirpy "clear" from Timsah.

It was his first word.

Uncle Alistair Jammpot spent a good deal of time strolling on the deck – guarded, of course – in hopes of spending the least amount of time possible with the Countess.

He had befriended serpents in the past. He thought of his friend Rodney, a good-hearted grass snake he'd met back home in England. Decent chap overall, but even Rodney startled him the first time he saw him sunning himself near the Brighton Pavilion. "After the first shock, I'm generally at ease with their kind," he thought. "Except the Countess. What a frightful thing she is."

The Tasty Rat lay at anchor, with no moonlight to show how far away the shoreline might be. He thought about giving the guard the slip and making a swim for it, but swim where? And how far? Were there crocodiles in this stretch of the river?

Lanterns rocked with the movement of the boat. He strolled beneath one of the overhanging booms and felt a raindrop land on the back of his neck. "I'll be dashed," he whispered. It was far too early in the season for rain.

He looked up to see if he could spot a rain cloud in the darkness and he froze at the sight of Ramses Faro crouched upon the folded sail, soaking wet and grinning down at him like the Cheshire Cat.

"What is it?" the guard asked.

"Not a thing," Uncle Alistair said without missing a beat.

When the guard reached the place where the raindrop fell, he looked up.

Nothing there.

Uncle Alistair continued his stroll, absolutely confident his particular friend would keep up – which he did.

Ramses used every form of sneaking, slinking, and skulking to climb and creep along the booms and ropes and awnings, perfectly silent, and nearly invisible, even to Uncle Alistair who knew he was there. They both tried to figure out a way to communicate, but how?

"Mind if I pop down below for a cup of tea?" Uncle Alistair asked the guard. He went to the cabin stairs, opened the door, and turned back. "Care for one?" The guard grunted and shook his head, and as expected, a soft voice spoke from the shadows somewhere above the cabin door. "Nose tap. Dive at signal. Nightjar."

"Understood," Uncle Alistair said to the voice in the shadows. When the guard looked up, he said, "Right-o, I understand you don't care for any tea. Be back in a jiff."

True to his word, Uncle Alistair reappeared on the deck a few minutes later. "Tea is brewing now," he said to the guard, and he resumed his nighttime stroll.

Ramses followed along on top of the boom and the furled sail. When Uncle Alistair sat down upon a deck chair, he crouched directly above him and looked out at the river. He opened his eyes wide and his black pupils nearly overwhelmed his golden-green irises to allow him to see the dark shape of the *Wind Cat* slowly gliding toward *The Tasty Rat*.

And then – movement below – his fur bristled at the sight of the Countess behind Uncle Alistair, uncoiling upon the cabin stairs with her tongue flicking in and out and her muscles rippling along her thick body.

She began to climb.

Before he could warn his friend, Uncle Alistair tapped the side of his nose. A second later came Felicity's birdcall from the darkness of the river. *Toc toc toc churrrrr!* The signal for Uncle Alistair to make his escape.

The Countess froze on the stairs.

Ramses tensed.

Without warning, Uncle Alistair sprang from the deck chair and ran past the surprised guard. Before the man could lift his rifle, Ramses leaped from the awning onto his back. The guard cried out and spun around - *and there she was!* The Countess! Racing over the deck with her neck hood extended and her single fang glistening in the lamplight!

Uncle Alistair leaped over the rail and dove into the river with barely a splash.

The cobra cursed and turned upon the cat still clinging to the guard. "There will be no ethcape for you!"

"You don't thay!" Ramses cried with a merry laugh. He sprang from the guard and sailed over the Countess. She lunged. Her head rose like the blunt tip of a spear to snag the cat in mid-flight, but she missed him by less than an inch.

Over the rail he went, did two twirling somersaults in mid-air, and splashed down into the river.

Earlier, Timsah had ferried him out to the dahabeeyah and was beside him in an instant. "To Jammpot!" Ramses said and he draped his paws around the little crocodile's neck When they floated up beside him, and before Uncle Alistair could ask him why he was clinging to a baby reptile, Ramses said: "Long story. His name is Timsah."

"How do you do?" said Uncle Alistair with a polite nod.

Behind them, the Countess bellowed for Pickelhaube. "Hermann-Düüfuth! They have ethcaped! Call the guardth!"

"Which way?" Uncle Alistair asked, treading water.

"We have a felucca." Ramses climbed higher upon Timsah. "And here it comes."

"Uncle Alistair!" Felicity called from the darkness.

"Over here!" Ramses cried.

A crack sounded – a gunshot – a whiz and a sharp pop of water beside them. Uncle Alistair's eyes widened with surprise.

"Shoot them both!" the Countess cried.

"Rather an overreaction, isn't it?" Uncle Alistair called to the dahabeeyah. "I mean, really Countess…*shoot* us? A bit much, if you ask me."

"Which no one did!" the Countess bellowed. She turned to the guards. "Now!" she shrieked. "Shoot them now! Aim for that cat!"

The guard dropped to the deck. He planted his elbows on the deck rail. He steadied his aim.

Before he could pull the trigger, there came a sudden splash from the river.

Straight up from the water it came, a thick black missile in an explosion of white spray. The guard shrieked when a set of jaws snapped around his arm. The rifle flew end over end into the river. The Countess recoiled in shock, and the black shape dragged the doomed guard from the boat to disappear into a churning froth.

"Crocodiles!" Uncle Alistair whispered, horrified. "Don't move, Ramses. Don't draw their attention."

Too late. A second shape appeared in the water, twenty feet away, like a submerged log rising to the surface.

A third joined it and they floated side by side, studying their prey.

"Almost there!" Felicity called and the felucca swung toward them.

"Hurry," Uncle Alistair whispered, not daring to raise his voice. He looked at Ramses, still clinging to the baby crocodile.

Ramses returned his anxious gaze and said: "Bit of a pickle."

"Climb aboard me," Uncle Alistair said. "You might make it to the boat."

"As will you." Ramses scrambled from Timsah onto Uncle Alistair's shoulder. "Here Felicity!"

The bow of the felucca cut through the black water.

The crocodiles surged toward them, sinking as they came. A bubbling ripple washed over Uncle Alistair.

The reptiles dropped below the surface. An upwelling of water marked their oncoming path.

Uncle Alistair cried out at a hard, violent blow upon his leg. He pushed against the snout of his attacker. The water thrashed and down he went, ripped beneath the surface with Ramses still clinging to his shoulder.

He pushed at the snout again, but his hands slipped upon the monster's hide.

Hauled to the surface again, he gasped "Jump Ramses!" and just when he thought he would be pulled under for the final plunge, he felt a second blow; a sharp, painful slam against his thigh.

It sent him up from the river in a fountain of spray. When he came down, he landed with a crash upon the deck of the *Wind Cat* with Ramses still clinging to his shoulder. Another splash followed and Timsah spiraled through the air. He smacked against the sail before tumbling down upon the deck beside them.

"My lower limb!" Uncle Alistair cried. "It's gone, I'm sure of it, I may require a tourniquet." He felt his right leg and gasped with relief to discover it there in one piece. "What on earth…?" He stared at Ramses, open-mouthed, and tried to say it again. "What on….?" but he couldn't manage it. Felicity leaped atop him with a cry of "Uncle Alistair!" and she wrapped him in her arms.

"What on earth…?" he said a third time, gazing wide-eyed at her.

"I don't know, and I don't care!" She burst into tears and buried her face into his shoulder. "You're safe!"

He tried a final time. "What on *earth* just happened?"

A gunshot rang out. A bullet chunked into the wooden boom above them.

They looked at *The Tasty Rat* now swarming with guards unfurling the sails and lifting the anchor. Another lifted his rifle for a second shot.

"Hold on," Sharrif called, and he hauled on the tiller.

A bullet struck the water behind them with a watery pop. Ramses sprang from the deck onto the boom and ran down its length before dropping beside Sharrif in the stern. "Do what you must," he said with a hearty shake of his fur. "Get us as far away as fast as possible."

"Where to?" Sharrif asked, and another shot rang out. This time, the bullet splashed far to the rear. The guards could no longer see them.

"North," Uncle Alistair said and, keeping low, he and Felicity crawled along the deck to join Ramses and Sharrif at the tiller. "To the Faiyum."

"Is there a reason for going there?" Ramses asked.

Uncle Alistair scratched him on the head and smoothed down his wet fur. "No reason at all," he said. "There is no Labyrinth. We have lost the sacred blue crocodile. We have no earthly idea what we might be looking for or what we might find."

"But still..." Ramses said with a wink.

"But still," Uncle Alistair repeated with a devilish grin. "On we go!"

IV.

AT THE FLAMINGO AND LIME

Ramses Faro

1

Countess Serpentina von Hyss raged from one end of *The Tasty Rat* to the other, furious over Alistair Jammpot's escape. She was especially furious because "that thneaky cat thabotaged all my planth!" The sight of the markings on the belly of the blue croco-dile enraged her further. "Hieroghlyphicth! All thothe thquiggleth! We'll never know what they mean now."

Pickelhaube dropped a sheet of paper on the table. The Countess squinted at it from behind her monocle. "*Hail Thobek, to thothe who path through the falthe portal.* Do you honethtly believe he tranthlated it correctly?" she yelled when she recognized Jammpot's translation of the crocodile's belly. "You're an even greater fool than I thuthpected."

Pickelhaube clenched his fists. His face turned red.

"Don't you *dare* turn thcarlet at me!" the cobra screamed. "Call the guardth, call the entire crew. Bring them here. We have much to dithcuth."

By the time the crew of *The Tasty Rat* gathered in the salon, the Countess had calmed down. She drew their attention to the blue crocodile and told them it was a key to unlock a vast treasure in the north, a key that was utterly useless until they found someone who could translate the symbols on the crocodile's belly and do it without lying.

"Not Jammpot, for I can no longer trutht him. And not that hideouth cat either," she snarled. "He ith more tricky and bloodthirthty than a thaber-tooth tiger. No, gentlemen, no. We mutht look to the young one, the girl. Felithity Jammpot. She told me she can read hierglyphth." She narrowed her eyes with sinister cunning. "The quethtion ith thith: how do we convinthe her to do it?" After a moment of silent meditation, her eyes widened again. "I have it!"

First, they must allow the little felucca to get ahead, maybe by a day, maybe more. They must allow Alistair Jammpot and his companions to believe they have left the *Tasty Rat* far behind.

In the meantime, they would make a stop to pick up some passengers near the city of Abydos. These passengers had a hideout far from the snooping eyes of the authorities. After she convinced their leader to join them, they would raise every sail and catch up to the felucca.

The crewmen glanced at each other, nervous. Who was this mysterious "leader"?

The Countess noted their anxiety and smiled with grim satisfaction. "An infamouth river pirate," she told them, "from the deep jungleth along the Congo River. Terror ith hith weapon of choithe and he will uthe it to attack without pity."

The ship's cook asked the name of this leader for he had known and heard of many river pirates over the years. The Countess' horrid grin widened when she said: "Umbalali."

"*The* Umbalali?" the cook said, and all color drained from his face.

"There ith only one," the Countess replied, and her hiss that wasn't a hiss nearly became a true hiss when she uttered his full and fearful name: "Umbalali the Thqueethe."

2

Sharrif was confident of his sailing abilities, even at night with no view of the river ahead. "We need to put some distance between us and them," he said. "You all try to sleep now. I'll keep watch until morning."

After an hour's snooze, Uncle Alistair moved to the stern where he sat beside the young captain and watched the passing river. They said little until the rising sun began to lighten the eastern shore and Sharrif's head began to nod.

"I'll take over now," said Uncle Alistair. "You sleep now, for as long as you like," he added softly, but he was sure the boy had not heard him. Without a word, Sharrif slumped against him. His head dropped upon his shoulder, and he settled in, fast asleep, and Uncle Alistair draped one arm over him while using the other to steer, with Ramses curled up, purring upon his lap, and Timsah on the seat beside him, and the waters of the Nile passing by, whispering, whispering gently against the hull.

Sharrif slept until the sun was fully up and then helped Felicity fish for breakfast. After a decent haul of perch and a catfish, Uncle Alistair sailed the *Wind Cat* up to an abandoned dock and they stopped to grill their fish and allow Timsah and Ramses to prowl along the shore.

Sharrif discovered that Timsah liked to chase sticks.

He gathered up a few and tossed them into the river and the baby crocodile moved them around with his snout. When the current swept them away, Sharrif tossed some more and again, Timsah moved them with his snout. "In the exact same way, in the exact same pattern," Sharrif said to the crocodile. "Is this a game?"

chirp

"What's it called?"

"Chomp," said the crocodile.

Back on board and once again under sail, Sharrif and Felicity tried to teach Timsah some new words while Uncle Alistair manned the tiller with Ramses crouched on the seat beside him.

"We are quite far ahead of the *Tasty Rat*," said Uncle Alistair. "I overheard the crew. They don't dare sail at night, not with the river as shallow as it is. This drought turned out to be a lucky break for us. I've never seen the water so low, nor the land so dry. Even so, we don't want to get too far ahead of them. Only a day or two at most."

Felicity overheard this and called back to them. "Why not?"

"They have that blue crocodile," her uncle returned with a frustrated snap of his fingers.

"Why do we need it?" Felicity asked. "We already know what the belly hieroglyphs say. Ramses saw your translation on the table in the Rose and Venom."

"You did not read it very closely," Uncle Alistair said to the cat beside him. "If you had, you would have realized it was all stuff and nonsense from beginning to end. 'Take a left at the baboon with three heads,' and that sort of thing."

"The only words I saw were 'false portal'," Ramses admitted.

"As luck would have it, those were the only true words in my entire translation. I *did* see something about a false portal on that blue croc's belly, and off I went from there, creating as wild a goose chase as possible. Didn't even bother to read the rest. I focused entirely on throwing that ridiculous serpent off the trail."

"Which means all we have to go on at this point is a false portal," Ramses said.

"Portal," chirped Timsah, and Sharrif scooped him up in his arms. "You'll be speaking full sentences in no time," he exclaimed with a laugh, and he kissed the crocodile on the top of the head.

Felicity sent him a smile as if to say, "What's gotten into *you*, oh crocodile hater?" but Sharrif ignored her. "What's a portal?" he asked.

Uncle Alistair craned his neck and looked over the bow. "It could mean several things," he said. "Look there, Sharrif. What is that up ahead?"

Sharrif scrambled to the bow and squinted into the sunlight. "An old boat. Looks to be abandoned. Caught on a sandbar, I think. You can sail around it easily."

They passed the derelict wooden boat and Uncle Alistair asked Sharrif to continue his watch on the river. "Don't want to get hung up on something before reaching Abydos."

"Are we going there?" Felicity asked with a hopeful grin.

"We are," Uncle Alistair said. "We've put enough distance between us and that ghastly cobra. I daresay we can manage a short stay in Abydos. Dinner at the Flamingo and Lime. How does that sound?"

"Wonderful!" Felicity exclaimed. "I'm getting a little tired of river perch." She swiveled around on the deck and told Sharrif he would like the Flamingo and Lime even more than the Café Happy Baboon. "They have honey-cakes too." Spinning around again, she reminded her uncle that he never finished answering Sharrif's question about the portal.

"A portal is another way of saying doorway or entrance," he said. "And false portal? Could be a false entry meant to mislead. The Pyramid of Hawara is a perfect example. My old chum Sir William Flinders-Petrie says it contains one devilishly difficult trick after another. Dead ends. Trapdoors. Obstacles. A massive stone block as large as this boat to protect the burial chamber from intruders. Which it did not."

"Thieves!" Ramses exclaimed as if he had never engaged in that sort of thing himself.

"Sadly, yes. Looted long ago. Sir William found only a single *uraeus** the thieves left behind." Before Sharrif could ask what a *uraeus* was, Uncle Alistair said: "A golden ornament worn by the pharaohs, shaped like a rearing cobra. Which reminds me…" He told them the Countess spoke of something called *The Book of Cobra*. Felicity said the Countess mentioned it to her too, back in The Rose and Venom. "What is it?" she asked.

"It's time we found out," her Uncle responded. "I wonder if there is a telephone at the Flamingo and Lime."

3

In the introduction to Lady Silvia Snogwitt's book, *Your Reptile's First Year: What to Expect,* she writes, "A toddler crocodile's first words will often be something simple, such as 'Mama' or 'Slash', but with loving care and patience, your leathery tot will be charming guests at the dinner table with 'Please pass the severed limbs,' and 'Might I trouble you for another gob of flesh?'"

Felicity and Sharrif had never heard of Lady Snogwitt's book and did not know the first thing about teaching a baby crocodile how to talk. They made a game of it by seeing who could get Timsah to repeat the words they came up with. As Lady Snogwitt might have predicted, Timsah would not repeat what they said but came up with different words of his own.

For instance, when Felicity instructed him to say "Dog", the little crocodile chirped and said, "Bite."

"No, Timsah. Dog. Say Dog."

"Gnaw."

After a few more tries with "water" (which Timsah repeated as "nibble") they finally got him to say "Kitty."

"Kitty," the little tot said. "Bite kitty."

"Two words in a row!" Felicity exclaimed and she clapped her hands. "He's making progress."

Ramses interrupted his nearby snooze. "Bite Kitty is not progress," he said, opening one eye. "Feed Kitty is progress." When Sharrif pointed out that the crocodile didn't even know what bite meant, Ramses closed his eyes again and said, "Let's hope he doesn't learn whilst in the vicinity of my tail."

Each time they stopped to roast a fish or whenever a lack of wind brought the boat to a standstill, Timsah prodded Sharrif into playing his favorite game of Chomp.

Sticks in the water.

Sticks pushed around with his snout.

Sticks washed away.

More sticks thrown and pushed.

They continued their crocodile language lessons too, and by the time they approached the ancient city of Abydos, Timsah could string together several words, and not all of them involving his jaws. "Old water city," he said, and Felicity told him, yes, the city beside the water was quite old indeed. "From the time of the pharaohs."

"Marrow," said Timsah.

They tied off the *Wind Cat* to a dock and Uncle Alistair tucked the reed sarcophagus under one arm. "Shall we?"

Dusty and dirty and hungry, they arrived at The Flamingo and Lime Hotel with Timsah hidden in the folds of Sharrif's robe (put there after Uncle Alistair pointed out the *No Crocodiles Allowed* sign beside the front door).

"Might you have a telephone in this establishment?" he asked the clerk at the front desk. When the clerk told him, yes, they had installed one only two weeks before, Uncle Alistair said, "What a jolly lucky break. And tell me, my good man...might you have three rooms available for the night?"

Felicity was overjoyed. She could barely hide her excitement when she leaned in close to her uncle and whispered, "Overnight? Really?"

"We are miles ahead of our slithery acquaintance," Uncle Alistair said. "I don't imagine you shall be too upset by the idea of a hot bath and a cool, comfortable bed."

"Wouldn't be upset in the least," she said and playfully bumped her hip against his.

"You shall have your own room, of course," said Uncle Alistair. "Sharrif and I will each have one as well. You as well, if you like," he said to Ramses.

"Not for me," the cat returned, and he told them he would be delighted to curl up at the foot of Felicity's bed, as always. "It's been ages since we've seen a proper bed."

"I don't mind sleeping on the boat," Sharrif said. "Someone should keep watch."

"Nonsense," said Uncle Alistair. He lifted the reed sarcophagus with the books inside. "We left nothing of value on board. We don't need a guard." He spoke to the clerk again. "We'll have three of your best rooms, if you please. With private baths."

"And big beds," Felicity said.

"The largest you have," her uncle agreed.

"And ceiling fans."

"Certainly, yes, ceiling fans. And shutters to keep out the noise of roosters. Possibly a terrace facing the river for morning tea. Might that be arranged, my good man?"

"It might, sir, yes," said the clerk with one eyebrow raised as he gazed with a touch of suspicion at the dusty, bedraggled travelers standing before him. Lowering his voice, and leaning over the desk, he asked, "And how might the gentleman care to pay?"

Uncle Alistair smiled. "The gentleman might care to pay with his account. Alistair Jammpot."

"Professor Jammpot!" the clerk said, straightening up at once. "I *beg* your pardon, sir, I didn't recognize you." His eyes darted to the cat perched upon Felicity's shoulder. "And you must be Ramses Faro."

Ramses answered with a friendly nod.

The clerk bent down, reached for something, and dropped a book upon the desk. They all recognized it as Ramses' latest, *Pawprints in the Sand*, with a picture of the great Feline Egyptologist himself on the cover, wearing sunglasses and standing in front of the Great Sphinx.

The clerk then set an inkpad down beside it. "Would you? I'd be ever so grateful."

"Certainly, my good man," Ramses said, and he hopped upon the desk.

He set his paw upon the inkpad. The clerk opened the front cover and Ramses autographed the front page over his name with a perfect paw print.

4

Felicity never complained about hardship or discomfort, but when offered a chance to spend a little time in elegant surroundings, she snapped at it as quickly as Timsah snapped at a minnow. Her bed was enormous, with crisp cotton sheets and pillowcases as white as newly fallen snow and a finely woven mosquito net attached to the canopy. The headboard and most of the furnishings were made of polished mahogany. Two fans spiraled above. A vanity with a mirror stood beside the door to her private bathroom. After catching a glimpse of herself in the mirror with her filthy dress and matted hair, she eyed the porcelain bathtub with delight and made up her mind at once to spend a good hour (or more) soaking in a steaming, lavender-scented bath.

Sharrif gazed at the bed in his room with more concern than delight. He had so rarely slept in a true bed. In the monastery, he slept in the stable upon a pile of straw. Even at Uncle Alistair's house in Cairo, he often chose to spend at least two nights a week in the back garden.

"They have bathrobes for us all," Uncle Alistair pointed out. "We can send our clothes out to be washed. Before we do, I'd like to make that phone call. Ramses can come with me."

"I'm going to take a bath immediately," Felicity said. "You should too Sharrif."

"I suppose so," he said without much enthusiasm, and he sniffed the sleeve of his black robe. "I don't think it's that bad." He sniffed again. "Is it?"

"Trust me. That robe is about to walk away on its own."

Labyrinth of the Crocodiles

Ramses and Uncle Alistair found their way to the hotel office and a wall phone with a crank and speaker. It would look like an exotic antique to anyone of later generations, but in those days in Egypt, it was the very latest thing. "Hope I remember how to use it," Uncle Alistair said.

Ramses hopped onto the counter with a single bound. "Who are you planning to call?" When Uncle Alistair said, "A certain narrow crawly sort of fellow," Ramses only stared. "Yes, you heard correctly," the professor said, and he began the complicated process of making a call from Abydos, Egypt to a grass snake in Brighton, England.

"Hello Rodney, is that you?" Uncle Alistair called into the phone. "Yes, yes, it's me – Alistair Jammpot, all the way from Egypt. How *are* you, old fellow? Fine, fine. And how is Evelyn? My word – seventeen!" He covered the mouthpiece with his hand and whispered to Ramses: "His wife laid seventeen eggs. All hatched, thankfully." Back to the phone again: "Say Rodney, I'm in a bit of a pickle. Might you know about a thing called *The Book of Cobra*? What's that you say? The British Museum? Hate to put you to the trouble. Oh, you're going there anyway?" Again, he covered the mouthpiece: "By coincidence, he's taking the 1:37 train to London this very afternoon. Has an appointment with his herpetologist." He thanked Rodney and said, "Yes, yes, tonight will be splendid. I'll await your call. Thanks ever so, Rodney."

He hung up the phone. "Now, there's a fine fellow if ever there was one. Says he has a chum in the British Museum who will allow him into the archives. Good old Rodney, I *knew* I could count on him."

The Flamingo and Lime was an oasis of comfort. Uncle Alistair, Sharrif, and Ramses cared little about lavender-scented soaps and freshly pressed bedsheets, but Felicity thoroughly enjoyed herself. After she sent her dress and Sharrif's robe out to be cleaned, she took her overly long bath and wrapped herself in a soft snow-white bathrobe and invited Sharrif to her room for tea.

Uncle Alistair retreated to his room to prepare for his own bath. When he took off his jacket, he dropped it on the floor, but picked it up again. "I say, Ramses."

Ramses called from the bathroom where he was playing with a stream of water coming out of the sink. "Yes, Jammpot?"

"Might you pop out here for a moment?"

Ramses pounced from the sink to the floor and trotted into the room. Uncle Alistair sat on a chair and turned his jacket this way and that, searching for a specific pocket. "Ah, here." He reached inside and pulled out a length of black cloth. "What do you make of this?"

Ramses hopped into his lap and pawed at it. "Looks like linen."

"Linen!"

"Very old linen from the looks of it," Ramses said. "If I had to guess, I would say it is a piece of mummy wrapping. Wherever did you get it?"

The professor's expression darkened. "Not possible," he said and held it up to the light.

Ramses pawed it again and snagged the corner with one of his talons. The linen slid from Uncle Alistair's hand and fell to the floor. "I don't know what else it could be," Ramses said.

"It certainly can't be mummy wrapping."

"Why ever not?"

Labyrinth of the Crocodiles

Uncle Alistair picked up the black cloth and dropped it into his pocket. "Because it came from the Nile. When I tried to push that crocodile away. Even in the terror of the moment, I thought it was odd, the way the beast's skin seemed to slip and come off in my hand. But it wasn't skin, apparently. What it is, I do not know, but it cannot – it simply *cannot* be a mummy wrapping." Ramses sat on the edge of the chair and looked up at him. His friend opened his mouth to say something, changed his mind and swallowed hard. "Could it?"

5

With their clothing washed and pressed, and their hair combed, and shoes and sandals and boots polished, and after Ramses spent a good half hour grooming himself to sleek perfection, the four travelers strolled into the dining room at the Flamingo and Lime with Ramses perched in his usual position upon Uncle Alistair's shoulder.

"Why the '*No Crocodiles*' sign?" Sharrif asked when the restaurant manager escorted them to their table. He had left Timsah floating in his bathtub and thought it unfair their friend couldn't join them for dinner.

"There was a...let us call it an incident, shall we?" the manager said as he pulled out a chair for Felicity. "Involving a large party of crocodiles who sang loud, inappropriate songs at their table one busy Saturday night, and our headwaiter who asked them politely to tone it down, may he rest in peace. Hence the sign."

Like the Café Happy Baboon, the busiest workers were the little monkeys running here and there, balancing trays, and sloshing pots of mint tea. The waiter (a man, not a baboon) told them his name was Claude from Paris, though no one believed he had ever set foot in France in his entire life.

He directed two little monkeys to bring three regular menus and one for "Monsieur Le Chat," as he called Ramses. "Would you like to start with le lemonade? Or un hot tea de mint?"

"Mint tea," said Felicity, and Ramses adjusted his spectacles and gazed at the cat menu.

"I'll start with the Assortment of Fine Garbage," Ramses said and twitched his whiskers. "Anything come with the Stewed Mice?"

"Would Monsieur care for Tail de Rat."

"No, don't care much for Rat Tail."

"Might Monsieur prefer le saucer de la crème?"

"Cream? Perfect," Ramses said and licked his nose with his tongue. "The catnip…imported?"

"Oui, Monsieur," said Claude.

"From where?" Ramses asked.

"Catalonia."

"Too strong. Any other?"

"Katmandu."

"Ah, very good. I may have the Katmandu catnip sorbet later, but let's wait on that.'

"Tres bien," said the waiter Claude. He turned to Felicity. "And you, mademoiselle?"

"Please ask someone else first," Felicity said, and she bit her lower lip. "I can't decide."

The waiter turned to Sharrif. "Monsieur?"

"You have chicken?"

"Certainly, monsieur," the waiter said, and he pointed at the menu with his pen. "How would monsieur like la chicken prepared? Boiled? Stuffed? Sautéed?"

Sharrif studied the menu, squinting and reading silently, "What are roasted peepers?"

"Monsieur?"

"It says Chicken with Roasted Peepers," Sharrif said. Behind him, two little monkeys who had overheard him could not contain themselves. "Haaaaaa!" one shrieked.

The other doubled over and screeched: "Roasted peepers!"

"Le silence!" the waiter Claude yelled, and the monkeys scurried away, trying to stifle their laughter but snorting through their noses. Before Felicity could help Sharrif out, the waiter rolled his eyes and said, "If monsieur would read carefully, monsieur would see the word is peppers. Not peepers. La chicken with roasted peppers."

None of the others at the table said a thing but looked at each other without letting Sharrif know they were looking at each other. Even so, he turned red from his chin to his hair. "I couldn't read it in this light," he said to Claude. "I'll have that. Chicken with roasted peppers."

A loud whoop of monkey laughter rang out from the kitchen and Sharrif's face turned a shade darker than before.

Ramses used his left paw to slap his menu shut and his right paw to adjust his glasses. "Forget the Stewed Mice, my good man. Chicken with Roasted *Peepers* for me too," he said, emphasizing the word, and the laughter in the kitchen stopped at once.

"A splendid idea," Uncle Alistair exclaimed. He closed his menu with as loud a snap as Ramses had closed his. "Chicken with Roasted Peepers for me as well. Felicity?"

"Peepers all around!" she cried loud enough for everyone in the restaurant to hear. She gave Sharrif a playful punch on the shoulder and he smiled and closed his menu with a shrug and said, "Chicken and roasted peepers for everyone," and Ramses leaned to the side as the waiter passed and whispered, "And a side dish of Assorted Garbage, if you please. Heavy on the fish heads."

After they finished dinner, the waiter Claude informed Uncle Alistair he had a phone call. "Must be Rodney," he said, glancing at his watch. "You all stay here, finish your dessert."

"Not me," Ramses said, and sprang onto his friend's back when he rose from the table.

Back in the manager's office, Uncle Alistair spoke loudly into the phone. "Any luck, old fellow?" There followed a string of: "Oh, I see...yes, I see...jolly interesting, that..." and he ended the conversation with a hearty, "Well done, Rodney. Truly, I cannot thank you enough. Give my love to Evelyn and the snakelets. Cheerio, Rodney."

He hung up the phone and sat on a stool. "I'll be dashed," he said and leaned back against the wall.

The cat blinked. "Well?"

Jammpot ran his hand over Ramses' back. "*The Book of Cobra* is a real thing after all," he said. "Apparently a great favorite with the serpent set. Devilishly tricky to translate. Rodney had to ring up his herpetologist two times over an issue of grammar. Not much in there about the labyrinth, I'm sorry to say. There was a bit about a hidden treasure, mostly offerings of gold and jewels to the sacred crocodile."

"Long since looted, I assume," Ramses said.

"*Possibly* looted." He felt the cat's back muscles tense. "Ah, that got your attention."

"How could there be a hidden treasure with no labyrinth to hide it in?" Ramses asked.

"How indeed?" Uncle Alistair gazed at the phone, puzzled. "Which brings us to a thing that makes no sense at all. He told me there was a phrase mentioned several times, but he could make no sense of it. Under is Over."

"'Under is Over," Ramses repeated. "Over as in over the hill? Or over as in finished?"

"He didn't say, and I doubt he knows. I doubt anyone knows. Except possibly…"

Ramses looked at him and nodded his head in the direction of the Nile. "Her?"

"Yes," Uncle Alistair said with a slow nod. "*Her.*"

6

Felicity adjusted the wick on her oil lamp. Ramses' spectacles lay beside it on the bedside table and when the flame brightened, the lenses did the same. She could have turned on the overhead electrical light, but she preferred the much softer lamplight when reading or writing (and she was doing both now). She held one of the books from Luxor in one hand and a pencil in the other. Ramses lay stretched out at her feet to take full advantage of the cool sheets and the air from the overhead fan stirring his belly fur.

Felicity picked up a sheet of paper with her notes. "Sobek," she read. "The one Sharrif calls 'Old Crocodile-Head'. Both good and bad, loved and feared. Protector of the Nile and responsible for the annual floods." She glanced over the paper at Ramses. "A difficult fellow."

"You'd be too if you had that unfortunate noggin."

Felicity laughed and glanced at her notes again. "A protector from the dangers of the Nile, but at the same time the cause of many of those same dangers. Uncontrollable. Ruled by instinct."

"Crocodiles do what crocodiles do," Ramses said. "Words to remember, especially when little leathery friend gets a little older and a bit bigger: crocodiles do what crocodiles do."

"Good point." She returned to her notes. "Sobek's temple centers were up north in the Faiyum Oasis and down south in Kom Ombo."

"And in the missing Labyrinth," Ramses said.

"All so interesting, isn't it?" She picked up the book again. "Sad too."

Ramses pawed her foot. He didn't really feel like playing but when she wriggled her toes, he couldn't help himself. "Why sad?" He swatted her big toe. Felicity did not answer. She stared at the book without seeing it. Ramses stopped playing with her foot. "Well?"

She lowered the book so she could see his eyes. "Sharrif can't read."

"Yes, he can," Ramses said.

"Well, yes, he *can* read, but he can't do it very well."

"He gets by."

"Ramses." Felicity closed the book and set it down. "Getting by is not enough if you want to be an Egyptologist."

Ramses sat up with his feet together and his tail curled over them in the pose seen in so many statues of the ancient cat deities. "Who said he wanted to be an Egyptologist?"

"Of course, he does," Felicity said, annoyed. "He's *with* us, isn't he?"

'Which means he wants to *be* one of us?"

"It's logical…don't you think?" Her annoyance had turned to doubt. "Isn't it logical?"

Without his spectacles, no glass came between Felicity and the sparkle of his golden-green eyes. "Last year we were with that herd of water buffalo up in the delta. Did you want to be one of them?"

She laughed and shook her head. "Why on earth would I want to be one of them?"

"We were *with* them, weren't we? You didn't feel an urge to wallow in the mud and swat flies with your tail?"

"Don't be ridiculous. Reading is not the same as swatting flies, and you know it. And fine. He doesn't have to be an Egyptologist. But an explorer of some kind…"

"Why?" Ramses asked.

"Because…"

"Because why?"

"*Because.*"

"Because *why?*" he asked.

"Because…" Frustrated, she dropped the book on the bed and said, "Because who wouldn't want to be an explorer?"

In the room next door, Sharrif couldn't sleep. The bed was too soft. The sheets were too crinkly. The pillows too fluffy. He tossed and sighed and turned about, lying first on one side, then another. "Impossible." He gathered up a blanket into a big ball and carried it to the bathroom where he set it down upon the tile floor. "You awake?"

A splash and chirp in the bathtub answered his question.

"Can I stay in here with you?"

Timsah floated in eight inches of water. Sharrif had set a stool on its side inside the tub in case he wanted to dry off for a while.

"Stay," the little reptile said, and Sharrif patted down the blanket and pushed it this way and that like a puppy circling on its bed before lying down. He pulled his bare feet up under his robe. "Much better," he said, and he wished Timsah a good night.

"Good bite," said the crocodile.

A narrow window above the bathtub sent a sliver of moonlight onto the wall. Sharrif stared at it, and thought, and stared at it some more. Finally, he sat up and leaned against the bathtub with his head resting on his folded arms. "Do you think I'm stupid?"

Timsah slashed at the water with his tail and climbed onto the stool.

"The monkeys in the restaurant think I am," Sharrif said. "They laughed at me. The waiter thinks it too."

"No me," Timsah said.

Sharrif reached into the tub and ran his forefinger over the top of the little crocodile's head. "That's because you're my friend.

Friends don't think other friends are stupid. But..."

chirp?

"But I think it too. Sometimes. I think I'm..." He didn't finish. "I can't read."

"What read?" the crocodile repeated, and Sharrif laughed. "Those black dots in that thing Felicity is always looking at. It's called a book. Those squiggles and dots all mean things. Sometimes it's hard to figure out what those things are. Sometimes they look like words. Other times, to me, they look like nothing but squiggles and dots. Like hieroglyphs. They don't make sense. Crocodiles are lucky. You don't have to read."

He dipped his finger in the water and made a lazy circle. "I guess it doesn't come easy for me." He lifted his finger from the tub and shook it. "I wonder if Felicity thinks I'm stupid too. And Ramses and Uncle Alistair. I wouldn't blame them. I love going on adventures with them, even though I can't always help. Sometimes I make things worse. Like when I thought I could find a tomb on my own. What happened? I fell down that Nilometer. But you know what?" he added when he noticed Timsah's head begin to droop. "I'm glad it happened. I would never have met you if it didn't."

He lifted the crocodile out of the bathtub and set him down on the blanket and he laid down beside him. "Maybe I should go back to the monastery," he said. "I was useful there. I didn't have to know about pharaohs or read books that are a hundred thousand years old. I wouldn't miss school or the owls, but I would miss my friends. I would miss you too."

"I come you with," the crocodile said, and he snuggled up close to the boy.

"The monastery is out in the desert a long, long way from where you belong."

"Belong you with," Timsah said, and Sharrif wrapped his arm around him and pulled him closer. "You belong me," the crocodile said, and as Sharrif began to nod off, the little crocodile whispered into his ear. "Pet." Sharrif didn't open his eyes when he whispered, "You're not a pet, you're a friend," and Timsah snuggled even closer and said it again, "pet," and Sharrif murmured "a pet *and* a friend" and sleep drifted over him and lowered him into its dark folds.

V.

UMBALALI THE SQUEEZE

Ramses Faro

1

They left the Flamingo and Lime and set sail upon the *Wind Cat*, refreshed, well-fed, without a care in the world. They had left the Countess and her dahabeeyah far behind – or so they thought. They did not realize *The Tasty Rat* was gaining on them by the hour. They also did not know the Countess had stopped along the way to pick up her mysterious passengers.

The crew of *The Tasty Rat* did all they could to avoid them. The ship's cook went into their quarters twice a day with platters of the most horrible food imaginable and came out each time with trembling hands and his face pale with fear. "Horrible," he whispered to a fellow crewman one late afternoon. "When will we ever be rid of 'em?"

The Countess startled him when she unexpectedly slithered into the pantry and said, "Thoon, very thoon. Major Pickelhaube caught thight of our prey up ahead. We will thoon catch up and our pathengers shall go forth to meet them."

The cook mopped his brow. "And when might that be, Countess?"

"Thith very day," the cobra said with a hiss that wasn't a hiss, and she glanced at the closed door of the passenger quarters with a hideous grin. "At thunthet."

And two hours later, sunset came…

Back aboard the *Wind Cat*, Sharrif and Uncle Alistair took down the sails and dropped the anchor for the night. They had no need to go ashore for they now had a small charcoal burner bought in Abydos to cook the day's catch.

They also had a few vegetables, a little sugar, a kettle to boil water for tea, and even some plates, forks and spoons (Felicity still had the knife found in the excavation site in Kom Ombo.)

When finished, they declared their first fish dinner back aboard the *Wind Cat* as fine as the one in the Flamingo and Lime. "Even better," Uncle Alistair said. He sat back against the mast and draped one leg over the other. "There we had no crocodiles to keep us company, whereas here…did you like your grilled minnows, Timsah? Or do you prefer them raw?"

"Grills," said the baby crocodile and he snapped up another as soon as Sharrif set it down upon his plate. "Nibble grills."

Uncle Alistair marveled at the crocodile's appetite. "Keep it up, and you'll be nibbling rather larger prey in no time at all." When he realized what he'd said, he grimaced and raised his eyebrows. "Let's jolly well hope you stick to minnows for the time being."

After a few minutes of contented silence with the boat gently rocking and all aboard lying about in lazy splendor, Uncle Alistair suddenly said: "Under is Over." He asked Felicity if she could guess the meaning of the phrase. She thought about it but had no idea.

"Neither do I," he returned. He told them of the conversation with Rodney and all he had learned about the *Book of Cobra.* "I'm not entirely certain I'd put much stock in a book composed by snakes, but there you go." He yawned and stretched his arms and he suddenly paused with his arms still in the air. "What's that?" He pointed up-river past the bow.

The sun had dropped. Shadows settled upon the Nile and darkened the riverbanks. Sharrif rose onto his knees. "It's a boat."

Felicity spun around, suddenly afraid. "The Countess?"

"No, too small," Sharrif said. He made his way to the bow where the anchor rope strained to hold the *Wind Cat* in place. A wooden boat drifted toward them, slow and aimless. No boatman sat at the tiller. No sail hung from its mast. Its hull appeared battered and scraped with age. "I know this boat," he said. "We passed it before we reached Abydos. Remember? It was caught on a sandbar. Must have broken free."

"It's not going to hit us, is it?" Uncle Alistair asked.

"I don't think so," Sharrif replied. "I can push it off if it gets too..." His voice dropped into silence.

Felicity looked from him to the derelict wooden boat and back again. "Do you see something?"

Sharrif shook his head. "No. Nothing. But..." He squinted and pushed his hair away from his eyes.

"But what?" Ramses asked. He stepped up so close to Sharrif that his fur brushed along the boy's ankle.

"The tiller moved against the current," Sharrif said. "It's sending the boat this way. It shouldn't do that if it's drifting."

"What does that mean?" Felicity asked without taking her eyes from the approaching boat.

Sharrif turned and looked at her. "Someone must be steering."

The abandoned boat drifted toward them in silence. Tiny ripples thumped against its hull but so softly only Ramses could hear them.

No one aboard the *Wind Cat* said a word. Sharrif climbed onto the boom. He held onto the mast and leaned closer.

"See anything?" Uncle Alistair asked.

"Something is holding that tiller," the boy said. "Looks like a rope. Someone must have tied it into that position."

"I don't care for this," Uncle Alistair muttered. "I don't care for this at all."

Sharrif suddenly pulled back to the mast with a gasp. "Something moved," he whispered. He rose to his toes on the boom, still holding onto the mast for balance. "I can't tell what it is. Looks like a rope but a rope wouldn't move on its own."

Uncle Alistair strode to the bow but could not see over the sides of the abandoned boat. "Ramses, might you scoot up the mast for a peep?"

"Right-o," said the cat and up he went.

Seconds later he clambered down again with his fur and tail twice their size. "Anchor!" he cried, and he jumped and landed with a thump at the bow. "We need to get it up. Now!"

"Come Sharrif!" Uncle Alistair exclaimed, and he sprang into action without knowing why. The urgency in Ramses' voice was all he needed.

"Felicity, you take the tiller," Sharrif said.

"And do what?" she asked, flustered.

"Hold it steady," he replied. "After the anchor is up, I'll raise the sails."

Sharrif ran to join Uncle Alistair at the bow. "What did you see?" he asked when he passed Ramses.

Before the cat could answer, the boy froze, staring. Uncle Alistair did the same, with both hands motionless on the anchor rope. Felicity craned her neck and was about to ask them what they saw when she, too, was shocked into silence.

What Sharrif thought was a rope tied to the tiller was not a rope at all.

It was a tail.

Its owner's head appeared, rising from the boat with streaks of white war paint on its face. It wore a necklace of lion claws and it stared with milky blue eyes as up, up, up it rose from the drifting boat.

"Python," Uncle Alistair whispered. "Look at the size of him! What the devil is he doing here, so far from his range?"

Ramses hopped onto his shoulder. "That isn't the Squeeze, is it?"

Uncle Alistair gasped beside him. "You *can't* mean Umbalali! I've heard of him, but never imagined...."

A second head appeared beside the first, a coal black spitting cobra with a spreading hood. It wore an eye patch over one eye.

"That settles it," Uncle Alistair said. "We shall have to make a dash for it."

He returned to the anchor rope but let it go when he heard a loud gasp from behind. It came from Sharrif, but instead of looking at the boy, his eyes shot to the derelict boat, now only twenty feet away.

"Oh, I say, that is rather alarming," Uncle Alistair murmured, shocked to see a band of serpents, jackals, monitor lizards and every manner of desert dwelling n'er-do-well rising in the boat with their mouths gaping and fangs and claws glistening. Among them and the largest of all rose the African Rock Python with the war paint, the only constrictor in the entire motley venomous crew.

"River pirates!" Ramses shouted, for he now understood who they were up against. Some wore ragged bandannas on their heads. Some had collars of filthy red velvet. Those with ears, like the jackals, had earrings. All had a sinister look in their eyes, shimmering with greed and wickedness.

Uncle Alistair picked up the charcoal burner. It had nearly gone out, but enough coals remained to explode into a fountain of sparks when he threw it. Light grey ashes plumed into a cloud. The burner hit the side of the pirate boat and fell with a splash. Cinders hissed into the water and the cobras and vipers hissed and their leader snarled the order to attack.

The crew of the *Wind Cat* shivered in horror when the first wave of snakes poured over the side of their boat. They plowed through the water in a wriggling mass, with heads bobbing and weaving and trailing low waves behind.

"Prepare to board!" came a second command from Umbalali.

The derelict boat drifted up close to the *Wind Cat* and some of the more slender serpents twined around ropes and pulleys like grappling hooks to fasten the pirate vessel to their prize.

"To arms!" Uncle Alistair shouted, though they had no weapons apart from the fishing poles and the silverware from Abydos. Uncle Alistair held out a fork. Sharrif did the same with a spoon. Ramses unsheathed his claws. Felicity stood the best chance as she held out the knife taken from Kom Ombo.

The pirates in the water boarded the *Wind Cat* in glistening coils. When the first one reached the deck, Ramses dropped from Uncle Alistair's shoulder and gave him a quick swipe with his claws. The snake twisted and would have sunk his fangs into him, but Ramses popped up to the boom as if he had springs on his feet and the pirate missed him by a hair. From there, Ramses leaped to the stern where Felicity crawled backward from another pirate with the knife in her right hand.

"And what has we here?' the viper pirate snarled as he swerved toward her. He wore a tiny tri-cornered hat and a rusty ring in his nostrils. "Think you is gonna run me through?"

"Come any closer and I will," she said, holding out the blade.

"And if she doesn't…" said a voice from behind. The pirate viper spun about and Ramses stood over him with a raised paw. "I will." He slashed the viper with a single strike. The rusty ring clattered to the deck.

"Aye, you filthy tiger!" the pirate howled. "That hurt, that did!"

The slender snakes strained, the pirate boat thudded up against the *Wind Cat*, and now there was no stopping them. The jackal pirates sprang from the small boat, howling like banshees, and they joined the reptiles, surging over the deck, hissing, spitting, and cursing up a storm.

"The Countess don't want 'em all!" boomed Umbalali, the only serpent remaining in the small boat. "Only the young one!" The pirates, like all pirates in all times, paid only half-attention to their orders. Like all pirates in all times, they were also far more interested in searching for loot or grog than taking captives. Felicity and Uncle Alistair stood with their backs against the mast and their weapons at the ready. Sharrif cowered in the bow, still hoping to pull up the anchor.

Umbalali saw him. "That one!" he thundered. He thrust his head toward the boy. His lion claw necklace clacked. Several slobbering mangy jackals circled around to meet Sharrif.

"Run Sharrif!" Uncle Alistair yelled. "This way!"

The boy leaped over the first jackal and raced over the deck, swerving to avoid the other pirates. When he passed the derelict vessel now up snug against the *Wind Cat's* hull, Felicity shouted: "Down!"

Sharrif ducked — too late! Umbalali the Squeeze, fully twenty-two feet long, shot over the deck.

Sharrif cried out when the python's mouth closed around his right arm. Before he could struggle, before he could call to the others, the pirate constrictor twisted and snarled him into a single thick coil. Umbalali hauled Sharrif struggling across the deck and carried him down into the pirate vessel with a crash.

A wild call sounded from the python. It was a high, eerie, trilling jungle cry. The pirate crew spun about wherever they were and raced from the *Wind Cat* onto the derelict vessel. "Away, you miserable maggots!" Umbalali commanded. "Away!"

The slender snakes released their hold upon the *Wind Cat*. Some of the sturdier vipers shoved off. The jackals bounded from the *Wind Cat* into the derelict, howling and yipping and screeching up a storm.

Timsah ran across the deck, chirping over and over, desperate to rescue his friend. He leaped for the pirate boat but missed and landed in the river.

Sharrif's arm rose from the squirming mass but dropped again, snatched down by one of his captors.

And then came a bell, loud and clanging, and the crew of the *Wind Cat* despaired at the sight of *The Tasty Rat* rounding a bend with all sails billowing and the writhing, howling, squirming pirate boat drifting into the middle of the river to meet her.

2

The pirates passed their terrified captive from hissing lizard to slobbering jackal to spitting cobra and, finally, to Umbalali. He gave Sharrif a quick, breath-stealing squeeze before dropping him onto the deck of *The Tasty Rat*. "We now take our share of the treasure, as promised," he snarled.

Labyrinth of the Crocodiles

"But…thith ith not the girl," Sharrif heard a voice say.

"You told me to capture a young one," the python returned. "You did not say boy. You did not say girl."

"I don't thuppothe it matterth," the voice said. "Bring him below."

Before Sharrif could react, a colossal man in a military uniform hauled him into the air as if he weighed no more than a small sack of rice. He tried to struggle but knew at once there was no escape. He lifted his head and caught sight of the *Wind Cat* in the distance, following. It was the last thing he saw before the giant carried him to the darkened salon down below.

Pickelhaube threw Sharrif to the floor. He rose to his knees. The giant grabbed him again, this time around the back of his neck. He lifted him squirming off his feet and slammed him down upon a chair. Pickelhaube kicked it. The chair slid across the polished teak floor and stopped with a jolt when Sharrif's chest banged up against a bare wooden table.

A wicker basket sat upon a chair on the opposite side. He stared at it with his chest heaving but did not say a word. Pickelhaube circled the table and, with a smirk upon his lips, he removed the lid from the basket.

Sharrif had heard about Felicity's first meeting with the Countess and he knew what to expect. It didn't help.

Her hairnet appeared first, then her monocle over one of her cold black eyes. Her wide horrifying grin came next and she said, "How do you do, my thplendid young fellow? I am the Counteth Therpentina von Hyth." Sharrif said nothing. Goosebumps rippled on his arms. He tried to swallow but couldn't. "And you are …?"

Sharrif said his name, though it sounded more like a mouse's squeak than a boy's voice. "Shar…Sharrif."

"Egyptian?" the cobra asked and Sharrif nodded. "I am pleathed to make your aquaintanthe." His grim hostess flicked her forked tongue once as if trying to taste his scent without letting him know. "I athume you know the reathon why you are here."

He shook his head.

She grinned again, wider than before. "Oh, but you do, you little thcamp. Your friendth will attempt to rethcue you. When they do, Umbalali and his crew of bucaneerth will take care of them. There ith no ethcape for you. If you try…" She looked him up and down. "A tathty morthel to thatithfy a thtarving python."

Sharrif leaped from his chair. He hoped he could make it to the door but Pickelhaube slapped his iron-tipped club against his chest and forced him back into the chair.

"Naughty little rathcal," the Countess said, and she nodded at her man-servant.. "Now then, Hermann-Düüfuth…"

Pickelhaube pulled a jangle of keys from his pocket and strode to a cupboard behind the Countess. After unlocking it, he withdrew the sacred blue crocodile and set it upon the table. The Countess gazed at it. "The time hath come to end thith, onthe and for all." She nodded at Pickelhaube. He turned the little blue crocodile onto its back to reveal the tiny hieroglyphs etched into its belly.

Sharrif's eyes widened. His heart thundered in his chest and another ripple of cold fear passed through his stomach when she fixed him with a deadly stare and said the two words he dreaded above all others.

"Read it."

Sharrif stared at the marks upon the blue statue.

"Well?" asked the Countess.

He began to sweat. "I can't," he whispered.

"You can't…what?" she asked, low and cold.

"I can't read it."

"Liar!" she snarled.

"I'm not lying!"

"You are a companion of Alithtair Jammpot and that…that horrible creature," said the horrible creature. "That thneaky feline! They would not keep you with them if you could not read it. Why would they? They have no uthe for a common, thimple-minded, ignorant, low-born peathant. Hermann-Düüfuth…" she said, and her meaning was clear.

Pickelhaube once again clamped his massive hand around the back of Sharrif's neck and he shoved the boy's face down upon the table. Sharrif managed to turn his head to the side so he didn't crush his nose, but his ear slammed onto the wood. He kept his eye closest to the table shut tight and, with the other partly open, he saw the giant push the crocodile closer to his face.

"Tell me what the hieroglyphth mean," the cobra commanded. "Read it!"

Sharrif whimpered when Pickelhaube applied more pressure. "I can't."

"Fool!" she spat out. "Releathe him."

The Major opened his hand and Sharrif sat up, gasping, and rubbing the side of his face.

"Thimpleton," the Countess snarled. "What good are you? I should give you to the pirateth to do with as they will. How is it that cat and the Jammpotth keep you with them? Remove that illiterate creature from my thight. Lock him away!"

Major Pickelhaube dragged Sharrif down the companionway and threw him into a small completely dark cabin. He heard the boy-fall and cry out, but he did not bother to check if he had hurt himself. He locked the door and rapped on it once with his club as a warning before returning to the salon to face the fury of Countess.

Ramses Faro

Inside, Sharrif stumbled up against a broken chair and banged his knee against a hard, narrow bed with no sheets or pillows or blankets, and no mattress. Only wooden planks.

He saw nothing apart from moonlight through a narrow air vent near the ceiling.

He pulled the chair up close and climbed onto it. The vent was too narrow to squeeze through. He rose onto his toes and saw the edge of the deck and moonlight sparkling on the Nile. Nothing more. No shoreline. No *Wind Cat*.

He dropped from the chair and sat down heavily upon the bed. Tears rose to his eyes and he tilted over on the wooden slats and pulled his knees up close to his chest. His kidnapping by the snakes, his imprisonment aboard *The Tasty Rat*, his bruises at the hands of Pickelhaube – any one of these was enough to bring tears to his eyes, but the thing that most brought them on was the stinging memory of her words.

Simpleton! Fool! Illiterate!

How she said them was brutal enough. *What* she said was more than he could bear.

He felt as if she had torn a bandage from an open wound. It was a wound he did not realize was so deep and so painful until she attacked him with her venomous words.

What was he *doing*? How could he have imagined that a common, ordinary camel boy had any business trying to keep up with the Jammpots?

Who was he?

An orphan, the same as Felicity. But Felicity came from known parents. Her father was a fighter pilot. Her mother was an elegant lady of London. But him? He had been dropped onto the doorstep of a monastery wrapped in a ragged shawl. No one had any idea who he was. No one had any idea who left him there. Even his name, Sharrif Aziz – the surname was borrowed from the Abbot of the monastery, and Sharrif given to him by the monks.

Who was his father? Who was his mother? His only known parent was a cold doorstep in the night, and his only inheritance a filthy shawl.

The owls at the academy looked down their beaks at him. He thought it was because he couldn't learn as easily as the others, but he now realized it was more than that. They saw him for what he truly was. A common, lowborn, no name, abandoned camel-boy.

A *fool!*

The Countess called him that out of anger. She lashed out with words designed to hurt him, and hurt him they did.

And now – there – imprisoned in the dark and utterly alone – the tears began to fall.

He hoped no one could hear him, especially Pickelhaube. He did not want to give that monster the satisfaction. He turned to face the hard, wooden slats and tried to hold back a sob but could not do it. He cried aloud for only a few seconds…but it was long enough.

Someone heard him.

Sharrif did not see him and did not know he was there, listening, until he stuffed his sleeve in his mouth to stifle another sob. That's when he heard a sound from somewhere above, a single whispered call drifting down from the air vent.

chirp

3

Back aboard the *Wind Cat*, they tried to make sense of all that happened. "Why Sharrif?" Felicity asked over and over. "Why would they take him?"

From the moment they began to follow *The Tasty Rat,* they missed their friend's sailing skills. They had to turn about several times and, once, Uncle Alistair grounded her upon a sandbar and had to jump into the river to push her off.

"Quite a beastly chore without Sharrif," Uncle Alistair muttered as he once again tried to untangle some of the lines.

"Everything's a beastly chore without Sharrif," Felicity said. "Hurry, Uncle. They're getting away."

They were desperate to keep the dahabeeyah in sight, especially after Ramses said to Uncle Alistair: "I know why they took him. The Countess believes you gave her a false translation of the crocodile's belly."

"Which I did," Uncle Alistair said.

Ramses nodded in approval. "And she thinks I would do the same, which I would. She has no choice but to force Felicity or Sharrif into making an accurate translation."

Felicity frowned in confusion. "But…but why would she do that? Sharrif has no idea how to read it."

Her uncle placed his hand upon her forearm. "She doesn't know that."

Over the next few days, they stayed as close as possible to *The Tasty Rat*. Uncle Alistair suspected the Countess would not order her crew to fire upon them for fear of hitting Felicity, the one remaining person who could help her.

"I know how to put an end to it," Felicity said one morning a little before noon, and Uncle Alistair studied her, curious. "We could call for a truce," she said. "We can offer to exchange Sharrif for me."

"Absurd!" her uncle exclaimed. "Do you honestly believe I would send you off alone to that ridiculous serpent?"

"Why not? He did." She pointed at Ramses.

"You did?" Uncle Alistair asked, rounding about to confront his friend.

Ramses lay nearby, snoozing in a sunbeam. "I might have," he said without opening his eyes. "In a manner of speaking."

"He did," Felicity insisted. "He sent me into her shop on my own and I survived."

"Honestly, Ramses," said Uncle Alistair. "Sending a helpless child into such danger."

"I'm not helpless," Felicity returned.

"No, you're not," her uncle agreed. "Poor choice of words. I meant...oh, dash it all, I don't know what I meant." He pointed at Ramses. "But the fact remains...that furry chap may take chances with your safety, but I cannot. I dare not risk it."

"There is nothing to risk," Felicity said. "I will translate the hieroglyphs for her – accurately."

Ramses swiveled onto his paws in a flash. He had been hard at work (lying in the sunbeam) thinking of a way to rescue Sharrif and send the Countess off on another wild goose chase. The idea of giving her what she wanted never occurred to him. "Why ever would you do such a thing?" he blustered.

"Because who cares?" Felicity cried and she threw her hands in the air in frustration. "You say we're on our way to an unknown adventure to a place that no longer exists, with nothing at the end of it. What difference does it make if she has a true translation?"

Uncle Alistair rubbed his temples with his fingers. "I suppose you're right."

"Oh, surely not, Jammpot!" Ramses exclaimed.

Felicity ignored him. "Then let me go," she said to her uncle.

Uncle Alistair looked at her with what Felicity thought was a sad smile and he turned away to gaze at the distant riverbank. Before she could ask, he said, "Bravest man I ever knew."

"Who?" Felicity asked, gently, as if she already knew the answer.

"My brother. Your father. He would be so very proud to know he had such a brave daughter. Your mother would feel the same. But bravery also has a brother and his name is foolhardiness. Your plan. I cannot tell at this point which one it is, brave or foolhardy, and so I must say no. It is not safe for a child your age."

Felicity's eyes flashed with anger. "My age?"

"Your age, yes," Uncle Alistair said.

"How old am I?"

"Not entirely certain," her uncle muttered after a long pause. "But…surely, you must be…what? Eight?"

"I'm *twelve!*" Felicity exclaimed, amazed he could never remember.

"Oh, yes, quite right. Old as the hills. But even so…even so…" Uncle Alistair struggled to come up with something. "Even so, as your guardian, I cannot put you in danger."

"Like this?" Felicity said, and she held out her hands as if to take in their surroundings. "Living for weeks on a boat while chasing cobras and river pirates?"

"This is different," Uncle Alistair said with a worried frown. He was losing the battle, and he knew it.

"What about the other times?"

"Other times, what other times?" he said, absolutely certain there were no other times.

Felicity quickly proved him wrong. "The quicksand in the delta," she said, tapping the fingers of one hand with the forefinger of another. "Or the time I was kidnapped in the desert. The airplane crash. The boat that sank off Alexandria."

"The water buffalo stampede," Ramses chimed in.

"Ramses please!" Uncle Alistair exclaimed. "I am attempting to be responsible."

"Scorpion in the sleeping bag," Ramses added. "Memorable."

"I've been in danger plenty of times," Felicity said.

"You have, yes," her uncle admitted. "But that was then. This is now, and I cannot allow it. Not at your tender young age of…eleven?"

"Twelve!"

"Ah yes, quite right. Twelve. Time flies and all that. Even so, I cannot allow such a thing."

"My age never stopped me before," she returned. "I've done all you've asked and faced all sort of difficulties and awful conditions. Isn't that so, Ramses?"

"It is. And without a word of complaint."

"There, you see?" Felicity said. Her uncle did not answer. "Honestly, there are times when you remind me of Aunt Ludmilla-Florence," she continued. He stiffened and she regretted her words at once. "No, no, I didn't mean that."

"Maybe so," he said in a soft voice. "But maybe I've given you too much freedom. I've been a frightful guardian. A terrible example. Irresponsible beyond measure."

"Oh no, Uncle, no," Felicity said, touching his arm.

He smiled at her again with the same sad smile. "My sister may be a humorless nightmare, but it is entirely possible she has more sense than I do." He threw back his shoulders and stiffened his spine. "Therefore, I must stick to my guns and say no. I cannot allow you to go on such a dangerous expedition on your own. And Ramses, don't you dare start scheming to send her into peril. We shall find some other way to rescue Sharrif."

Felicity wouldn't budge. "And what will you do if I jump ship without your permission?" She turned to Ramses. "Or yours."

Ramses raised his eyebrow whiskers in mock horror: "Mutiny!"

"I expect you to listen and do as I ask," said Uncle Alistair. "For once. Is that clear?"

She gazed at the receding dahabeeyah but did not say a word.

"Is it clear, Felicity?" he asked.

She nodded without looking at him but still did not say a word.

"Very well then," said her uncle. "Let us now put our heads together and come up with another, less dangerous plan."

4

The Countess tried several times to terrify Sharrif into reading the hieroglyphs. Nothing worked, and she came to believe he had told her the truth. He could not translate the blue crocodile. The pirates had kidnapped the wrong one.

She called for a war council in the salon.

The pirate Umbalali slithered in, all twenty-two feet of him, wearing his warrior chieftain's ceremonial dress. "Very imprethive," the Countess said, admiring his lion tooth necklace, the leopard-skin cape tied around his neck, and a headdress of bright red feathers.

"Tea?" the Countess asked.

"Blood," said the python.

She pursed her thin snake lips and cleared her throat. "Afraid we're out at the moment." Even the Countess had limits and serving blood at breakfast was one of them. Her guests would have to make do with tea and a platter of rodent scones.

"Gerbil marmalade?" she asked, but they declined.

While Pickelhaube spread a dab of gray marmalade on her scone, she attempted a bit of polite chatter before getting down to business. "Tell me," she said, "how did a magnifithent python chief of the Congo jungle find himthelf the leader of a band of Egyptian pirateth?"

Umbalali the Squeeze snarled, "I have no time for small talk."

Labyrinth of the Crocodiles

"Thomething to keep in mind," said the Countess with a sniff. "No thmall talk for the large python."

"I have come to claim it," said the python.

The cobra blinked. "It...?"

"My share of the gold," the python said with a sneer.

She blinked again behind her monocle. "Not pothible. After all, we *do* need to dithcover the gold before you can claim it."

The python flicked his tongue. "You promised me gold when I brought the young one."

"But I meant a girl young one, a thugar and thpice and everything nithe kind of young one. I did not mean a thnaketh and thnails and puppydog tailth kind of - "

"Enough!" the python said, and she reared back, startled. "I want the gold," Umbalali snarled. "Now!"

"Impothible," the Countess said again. "You may thearch *The Tathty Rat* high and low and you will not find a thingle thpeck of gold. We cannot get it until we find the Labyrinth."

The pirate chieftain stared, and quick as lightning, he shot across the table. Scones and fine china and jars of gerbil marmalade crashed to the floor. The Countess squealed with shock and backed into her chair. Umbalali stopped within an inch of her face.

"You promisssssssed," he said with a murderous hiss.

"I do not have it," she said in a stricken whisper. She explained the situation, how the boy was to reveal the secrets written upon the blue crocodile. "But that fool of a boy cannot read," she stammered. "You kidnapped the wrong one."

Umbalali twisted and the weight of his body snapped the wooden table legs and sent the table crashing to the floor. "Bring me the gold within two days or you die within my coils."

"Die! Really? *Die?* But...but...but mightn't that be conthindered a bit exthtreme?"

Ramses Faro

"Die!" the python snapped. "This I swear to you. You have two days. And do not try to slither away. I will follow wherever you go." Umbalali circled around to the door. "Until then, I will make do with the boy. I'll not need to feed again for a month."

The python departed and the Countess slithered back and forth in the salon, frantic. "Whatever will I do?" she asked Major Picklehaube. "If Umbalali thwallowth that fool of a boy, we'll never get the Jammpotth to help. Releathe him. We do not want him trapped in a thmall cabin with that python on the prowl. I need that girl Felithity. I need her to read that…that…" She thrust her head toward the blue crocodile. "That *thing* that hath cauthed me no end of grief. Go now, Hermann-Düüfuth. Let the boy wander the boat, but thend a guard with him. Tell the guard to never let him out of thight, not for a thecond. And try to talk thome thenthe into Umbalali if you can…oh, that'th right, you can't talk. Draw pictures. I mutht think of a plan."

5

The cook unlocked Sharrif's door. "Here you go, lad." He set down a plate of scones and a cup of tea. "These is real scones, not the ones the snakes eat." He shuddered and glanced back into the hall. "You can't imagine what they eat, the devils. I hate reptiles, I truly do. Them jackals ain't much better, but at least they got fur, such as it is."

Sharrif had pulled Timsah deep into his robe when the door opened. The cook had no idea he was only inches from another hated reptile.

"I'm to leave this door unlocked," the cook said. "Don't ask me why, 'cause I don't know." He looked out into the hall. "Word

Labyrinth of the Crocodiles

has it the Squeeze has his eye on you." He tapped his forehead as he backed out of the cabin. "Don't do nothing foolish. Keep your wits about you. Watch your back."

The cook had followed the orders Pickelhaube wrote down, exactly as commanded. What he did not do was send an armed guard to follow and protect Sharrif. He did not know that was part of the order. For some reason, it had not been included in Pickelhaube's note.

After wolfing down the scones and gulping the tea, Sharrif tucked Timsah deeper into the folds of his robe and left the cabin. "If you see that big snake before I do, let me know."

He met no one in the hall or on the stairs. When he stepped outside, he saw only the crew members and a few vipers lounging about in the warm sunlight. He strolled along and studied the lines, the ropes, the sails; and quickly realized the dahabeeyah operated much the same as a smaller boat.

After taking two turns around the deck, his heart quickened to see the *Wind Cat* round a bend behind. So they hadn't abandoned him after all.

Sharrif went to the bow. When he passed the cabin stairway, his heart leaped at the sight of Umbalali coiled in a glistening mound at the foot of the stairs. The monstrous Pickelhaube sat on a step before him. His hands fluttered and moved and the snake lay before him, entranced by whatever the Major might be telling him in whatever mysterious wordless language they were speaking.

Sharrif darted away before either of them noticed he was there. After another look at the felucca (now almost even with the dahabeeyah but on the far side of the river), he glanced at the water ahead. A large sandbar sat right in the middle of the river, like a long island bare of any grass or trees. As they approached to pass it on the left, he strolled up to the captain standing at the ship's wheel. "I've never sailed a boat before," he said in Arabic.

143

"You sailed that felucca," the man grunted. "I saw you."

"I only did what they told me. I couldn't figure it out on my own. I'm not that smart." The Captain didn't respond. "What's that thing?" Sharrif asked.

"It's called a wheel, dunce. The wheel turns a rudder and the rudder turns the boat."

Sharrif pointed up. "Is that the rudder?"

"Don't be a fool," the man snarled. "That's a sail."

"Oh, I see," Sharrif said softly. He looked past the bow. They approached the sandbar. It now passed along their right, starboard side. On the opposite far side of the sandbar, the *Wind Cat* bobbed along, trying to keep up. He rose onto his toes and studied the water ahead. A sudden patch of ripples swept over the river. He knew that meant a strong gust of wind was heading their way.

The Captain was studying the *Wind Cat* and didn't notice it. Sharrif doubted anyone aboard the dahabeeyah noticed it. He stepped back and whispered something into his robe.

He approached the Captain again. "Can I steer it?" he asked without taking his eyes from the water ruffling in front of the bow.

The Captain snorted a gruff, "No."

The fluttering gust approached, strengthening. Sharrif had to get to the wheel before it arrived. He asked again if he could steer and again the Captain said no.

Sharrif took a deep breath. He had no time. He whispered into his sleeve and then, "What's this?" he asked.

The Captain turned.

Sharrif thrust his arms from his robe with Timsah clutched in his hands. The man gasped with shock and the crocodile snapped.

The Captain howled. "Oh, by doze!" he yelled, sounding more like he had a stuffy nose than a crocodile clamped onto it. He spun around in circles, yowling. Timsah spun too, with his tail straight out.

Sharrif leapt to the wheel and turned it. "Hang on, Tim!" he cried. The gust of wind washed over the bow and struck with a sudden *whoosh* in the sails. The booms swung over the deck. The masts whined. The boat heeled onto her side. The Captain reached for the wheel but Timsah tightened his grip and "By doze!" he cried again. "Get dis devil off by doze!"

The dahabeeyah slammed into the sandbank. Sharrif braced himself against the wheel and the captain tumbled past him. A sound of breaking dishes came from below. One of the pirate vipers dropped from the rigging and slapped down beside him.

"Come Timsah!" Sharrif cried and he snatched his friend from the Captain's nose and ran across the deck. "Man overboard," he whispered with a grin, and he stepped up onto the rail, and over he went in a grand, thoughtless, leap of joy.

6

"Felicity, don't!" Uncle Alistair cried but too late. The moment she saw Sharrif leap from *The Tasty Rat*, Felicity forgot all about her promise to her uncle and dove without thinking from the deck of the *Wind Cat*.

Uncle Alistair swung the tiller, but he was so flustered he turned it the wrong way. Ramses perched on the bow, ready for a jump as soon as he turned it back again.

Felicity rose from the shallows and waded ashore. Her feet sank into the mud and made a sucking sound with every step. "Sharrif!" she called. "This way!"

"I dropped Timsah!" he called from the other side of the sandbar. The hull of *The Tasty Rat* had run aground deep into the sand. He felt through the muddy water beside it, searching.

"Hurry!" Felicity called. She ran onto the sandbar but stopped dead at the sight of a viper rising over the deck rail directly above

Sharrif. It was the same viper that fell from the rigging when the boat slammed ashore. It oozed over the rail, lowering toward Sharrif with its jaws gaping. "Above you!" Felicity called.

Sharrif looked up. A shudder ran down his back at the sight of fangs and the gaping pink mouth, lowering. "Timsah!" he called, and he splashed in the water with his hands, searching for his friend.

"Hurry, Sharrif!" Felicity called. "Run!"

"I can't find him!"

The viper smacked his jaws together, eager for a bite. "Stand still now."

Felicity called again: "Run, Sharrif!!"

"Go on, try it, I'll still catch you," said the viper. The heaviest part of his body slipped over the rail. He dropped and landed like a ghastly scarf over Sharrif's shoulders, weighing him down. The boy cried out and shoved him off before the viper could tighten his grip. The viper pirate landed in the water but immediately splashed up again, with his head nearly at the same level as Sharrif's. "Should have run like she told you," he said with a mocking, taunting grin, and he reared back, preparing for a lethal bite.

Sharrif cried out. The viper struck. Its fangs barely grazed his neck when a missile shot from the churning water and knocked the serpent off balance.

"Timsah!" Sharrif called, and the little crocodile dropped back into the water. In a split second he splashed up again and gave the viper a nasty bite on the snout.

"Ow, you crocodile swine-face hyena rat!" the viper yelled, not knowing exactly what had attacked him and throwing out some possibilities.

"Run!" Felicity called again. Sharrif pulled the crocodile into his arms and dashed toward her. They met in the middle of the sand-bar. "This way!" she cried and grabbed him by the arm. "Run to Uncle Alistair."

"What about you?"

"I'm going to go to them. They want someone who can read…" She meant to finish with the words "those hieroglyphs" but she stopped in mid-sentence and Sharrif heard only "They want someone who can read."

She pointed over his shoulder. "Look!"

The eerie jungle call trembled in the air and the full band of pirates began to drop over the side of the dahabeeyah: snakes, lizards, jackals, the whole scurvy lot of them.

They twisted in mid-flight to land belly or paws down in the water. When Umbalali's turn came, his head with his red-feathered headdress was already on the sand while his tail was still aboard the boat. His body dropped with a mighty splash. "The boy is *mine!*" he called, and on the pirates came.

They swerved and raced and crawled over each other in their mad dash onto the sandbar.

It was hopeless. Sharrif and Felicity could not outrun them. They had no place to hide. They turned to face their attackers.

Aboard the *Wind Cat*, Uncle Alistair jammed his fingers into his hair, frantic. "I can't get the boat to go where I need it to go. Oh, Ramses, what can we do?"

"Only one thing," said the cat and he sprang from the boat into the river. He splashed ashore and streaked across the sand. When he reached his two young friends, he stood in front of them and faced the oncoming pirates with his tail up, back up, fur at attention and all four feet fully armed with claws. "Run!" he ordered. "To the boat. Go!"

Umbalali led the charge with a hiss as loud as a battle cry. The others took up the call and on they came, slithering over the sand.

"Go *now!*" Ramses cried, but his friends could not force their feet to move. Felicity threw her arms around Sharrif and buried her face into his shoulder. Sharrif did the same, holding her with one arm and clutching Timsah with the other.

Uncle Alistair aboard the boat could not bear to see what he knew was coming, and he too turned away.

Ramses, alone, did not close his eyes. He glared at the oncoming pirates with a fierce, deadly glare that widened in shock at the sound of an unexpected roar from behind. He spun around in time to see the river split open beside the *Wind Cat*.

Three black figures tore out of the water.

They raced over the sand with mouths agape and blackened teeth exposed. Their skin streamed around them in tatters.

Ramses leaped onto Felicity's shoulder as they passed, and Felicity and Sharrif hid their eyes and clung to each other and listened in terror.

Roars! Hisses! Yowls!

Cries of dread!

Snarls of fury!

They heard and felt them all, and when the sounds faded and they opened their eyes, they discovered to their shock that they stood alone upon the sandbar.

The pirates had scattered. The jackals had raced to the far ends of the sandbar. The slower serpents and lizards had dashed back into the water beside *The Tasty Rat* in a panic and were now streaking through the water toward the distant shore. Even the fearsome Umbalali had taken flight. His feathered headdress swerved back and forth, and he lifted a wave of white water before his snout in his dash to safety.

Trailing bubbles marked the trails of their enemies, now following. Once in a while, they plucked one of the snakes down beneath the churning water, never to be seen again.

Uncle Alistair finally managed to sail the *Wind Cat* closer to the sand bank. "This way!" he called. Felicity ran to him with Ramses upon her shoulder. Sharrif did the same with Timsah in his arms. The boy reached the boat first and Uncle Alistair hoisted him aboard. Felicity strode into the water.

"Up we go," Uncle Alistair said but Ramses stopped her. "Not yet," he said, and he looked back at *The Tasty Rat*.

"Come Felicity – come!" Uncle Alistair urged, holding out his hands. "You too Ramses. They may return."

Ramses ignored him. He hopped from her shoulder to the sand at the river's edge. Felicity waded out of the water and stood beside him.

Uncle Alistair fell to his knees and slapped the side of the boat to get their attention. "What on earth are you *doing*?"

"The time has come to put an end to this," the cat returned. "We shall go with Felicity's idea."

"My idea," Felicity said, and her gaze drifted away, puzzled. "Which was...."

"I need something white." He lifted his paw and stroked the hem of her dress. "Would you mind terribly...?"

Without a word of complaint, she tore a long strip of white lace from her dress.

"Tie it to the tip of my tail."

She knelt in the sand and did as he asked. When she finished, Ramses rubbed his cheek against her hand. "Join your uncle now. I'll be back in a jiff."

"Let me go with you." She ran her hand over his back to the tip of his tail where she made sure the lace was secure (but not too tight.)

"Not this time," he said and once again rubbed his whiskers against her wrist. "A jiff. That's all it will take. Off you go now."

After Uncle Alistair lifted her aboard, Ramses padded across the sandbar with slow, deliberate steps and his tail straight up.

A light breeze lifted the lace, and he stopped before the stranded *dahabeeyah* with the white streamer fluttering.

Pickelhaube appeared on the deck.

His walrus mustache gleamed in the sunlight but could not hide his stern scowl. As usual, his helmet shadowed his eyes.

Ramses called up to the giant. "Hear me, Pickelpuss. This is not a flag of surrender. Do you understand?"

Pickelhaube nodded but his expression did not change.

"Enough is enough," Ramses continued. "You have the sacred crocodile. We have the ability to read the words upon it. I have come with this flag to call a truce. A *truce*, Pickelpuss, which means no fangs, no claws, and no river pirates. Does the Countess agree?"

Pickelhaube left the deck. Ramses waited alone on the sandbar for nearly ten minutes before the Major reappeared and looked down from *The Tasty Rat* and nodded sharply, once.

"Very well then," Ramses said. "Lower a rope. I am coming aboard."

VI.

INTO THE FAIYUM

Ramses Faro

1

Ramses sat upright on a chair in the salon with his tail wrapped around his paws. The flag of truce trailed from its tip nearly to the floor. The Countess lay coiled across the broken table with Pickelhaube standing guard behind her, staring with his usual hostile stare.

"Let's get down to business," Ramses said. "You stole the sacred blue crocodile from us in Kom Ombo." The cobra smirked but said nothing. "Jammpot gave you a false translation," he continued. "You suspect I would do the same."

The Countess corrected him. "I more than thuthpect. I am thertain of it."

"I have an answer to that. You can meet with us one at a time. Alone. We will each tell you what the hieroglyphs mean. If we all give the same answer, you'll know we are telling the truth."

"And after you know the meaning of the hieroglipth, you will try to dithcover the treasure without me."

"Impossible as long as you have the blue crocodile," Ramses returned. "After all, it is supposed to be a key…to *something*, though no one knows what that something might be."

After a long suspicious pause, she nodded and Pickelhaube set the crocodile down on the table. Ramses crouched beside it, adjusted his spectacles, and flipped it onto its back.

After studying it for some time in silence, he read the inscription aloud: *"Hail Sobek! To those who pass through the False Portal. I am a crocodile immersed in dread. The secret is opened for those who follow the birth of the King. I know the name of he who guards the golden treasure. Sobek is the name of the gate-keeper. He waits to attend the Petsuchos, the Son of Sobek, who shall bring forth the water of death and water of life."* Ramses sat back. "Nothing more."

"But…but there *mutht* be thomething more!" the Countess sputtered and she glared at the blue crocodile as if expecting it to apologize. "Follow the birth of the king…gate-keeper…Thon of Thobek. It meanth nothing. Gibberith!"

Ramses twitched his whiskers. "It sounds like gibberish, but it has meaning to those who understand the ways of the ancients."

"You could be lying, the thame way Alithtair Jammpot lied."

"I could, yes. So let us retreat to the middle of the sandbar. You, me, and Pickelpuss."

Pickelhaube clenched his fist around the handle of his club.

"I thaid you *could* be lying, but I thuthpect you are not," the Countess said after a long pause. Ramses noted the relief in her voice. She glared at him again, this time without suspicion or anger.

It was a stare to let him know she had something to say but did not dare say it.

"Where are my mannerth?" she suddenly asked, and she told Pickelhaube to step out to the galley kitchen and bring back a dish of fresh cream for their guest. As soon as the giant left the salon, Countess von Hyss curled down close to the table. "Umbalali the Thqueethe," she whispered. "I do not trutht him. I do not trutht you either, but you I can control. Him, I cannot."

"Why couldn't you say this in front of Pickelpuss?"

She tilted her head, startled by the question. "I don't know," she said, confused. "It may thimply be a matter of too many cookth thpoil the thoup." She told him of Umbalali's threat to kill her if she did not give him the gold. "Were he ten feet shorter, I'd think my fang into the filthy worm without hethitation, but the brute ith twenty-two feet long if he'th an inch. Let me come with you to the Faiyum."

Ramses blinked with surprise. "*With* us!"

"Awkward, yeth, but I thee no other way to avoid Umbalali. You mutht avoid him too. I did not mention thith before...that boy. The python wantth him."

"For what?"

"Thupper."

Ramses shuddered. "You and Pickelpuss joining us," he muttered, mulling it over. "Under a flag of truce?"

"Until we reach the Faiyum. There it will end, and we go our theparate wayth."

"Umbalali may follow."

"Wrong, cat. Not may follow – he *will* follow. Therefore, we will join you in thecret, in darkneth, well after thunthet."

The door banged open and Pickelhaube entered with a dish of cool cream and set it down before Ramses. "When finished, you are free to go," the Countess said. Pickelhaube looked at her, suspicious. "Yeth, Hermann-Düüfuth, I have dethided to releathe him," she continued. "Furthermore, I have dethided we will work together."

"Starting when?" Ramses asked after sniffing the cream for traces of poison. "And where?"

"Tonight. On the river. At midnight."

2

"Hail Sobek!" Ramses began. Uncle Alistair and Felicity listened closely as he repeated the memorized translation for a third time.

"What does it mean?" Sharrif asked from the tiller.

"It's a spell," Felicity explained, "and most spells don't make sense at first."

"I don't think they'll make any sense to me at all - ever," Sharrif said softly to Timsah on the seat beside him.

They had anchored the *Wind Cat* about a mile from the stranded *Tasty Rat*. Ramses took up a position at the bow. A little after midnight he saw movement within the deep shadows of the night, and in a low voice he said: "She's here."

The others grew tense.

Uncle Alistair lifted the lantern.

The wooden boat used by the pirates loomed out of the darkness. Pickelhaube manned the tiller, cold and stony. The basket lay at his feet with its lid in place and (they assumed) the Countess coiled inside.

Sharrif still bore the red marks of the table on his face and had more reason than the others to fear Pickelhaube. Even so, he grabbed the bow line of the drifting boat and tied it at the stern, and there they sat for the rest of the night with all aboard the *Wind Cat* taking turns at keeping watch on the wooden boat.

The following morning, they raised the anchor and so began their long, oppressive voyage upon the Nile, towing their dreadful cargo at the end of twenty feet of line.

Pickelhaube sat in the wooden boat and never took his eyes off them. No one aboard the *Wind Cat* ever saw him sleep – if he *did* sleep, he did it without closing his eyes, which seemed even creepier and more disturbing than if he hadn't slept at all. During the daylight hours he shaded himself and the wicker basket with a black umbrella. At night he sat with it furled upon his lap like a saber. Both day and night he sat in the same position without moving, silent and staring.

Sharrif had the worst of it as he offered to handle the felucca the entire time they were under sail. Uncle Alistair tried to help, but the boy insisted. "You can all talk about the words on the crocodile belly," Sharrif said. "I can't help with anything like that."

When they stopped at night, he kept to himself or played Chomp with Timsah. Felicity tried to play too but grew impatient after the first round. "I don't understand the point," she said. "You throw the sticks to the same places and he does the same thing over and over."

"I don't think there is a point," Sharrif explained. "We've done it so often I could follow his trail from stick to stick with my eyes closed." Felicity tossed a stick and watched Timsah push it to its usual position. "I know it's not fun," Sharrif added, "but maybe he doesn't think our games are fun."

"He hasn't tried. Maybe he'd like cards. Ramses loves cards, especially rummy. I don't know why Timsah can't give it a go."

"Because not everyone can keep up with you."

Felicity stared in surprise. What a strange thing to say. "I would never expect him to keep up. Not at first."

"Why not?"

"Because he's a crocodile!" she said with a laugh. "I would never expect him to keep up."

"Don't let him hear you say that."

Felicity smiled. "I remember when you had no use for crocodiles."

"I still don't. Not big ones."

"Little ones?"

"No." He looked over the side of the boat. "Only this one."

"And when he becomes a big one?"

Sharrif watched Timsah make his slow wandering path through the floating sticks. "I don't know. Maybe things will change. Maybe friends don't stay friends forever."

3

The Faiyum Oasis began as a natural depression in the desert sixty miles south of Cairo. The first pharaohs of the Middle Kingdom built a canal to link the depression with the Nile and the waters rushed in to form a vast lake called Lake Moeris. By the time Amenemhat III came to the throne in 1860 B.C., the Faiyum had become a lush, vibrant land of green fields, and a home to birds and plants and numerous villages. Long after the pharaoh's reign, the area fell into disrepair. New canals were dredged and they flooded or damaged many of the pharaoh's works. Some of the older canals filled in or dried up. Temples and pyramids were looted and torn apart. Some disappeared. The green fields remained, and the birds and flowers, but the majesty of Amenemhat III's day faded away, never to return.

When the *Wind Cat* pulled into a narrow canal below the village of Beni Adi, they discovered the water so low they could only go a mile or so before they ran aground and had to abandon her. "I say, Pickelhaube," Uncle Alistair called to the wooden boat floating behind. "We are at the edge of the Faiyum. I had hoped to reach the main canal of Bahr-Yussef, but it's not to be. Once ashore, we should discuss the truce and whether we shall end it here or not."

Pickelhaube stepped out of the boat into the knee-deep water (knee-deep for him, but nearly waist-deep for Felicity and Sharrif).

He carried the wicker basket up the steep bank of the canal, set it down, and opened it.

The Countess emerged, blinking in the sunlight, and took in their surroundings. "Well, well, the famouth Faiyum," she said with a disdainful sniff. "Thimply breathtaking. Now what? We are out of danger from Umbalali. Do we thtay together? Or do we end the truthe and go our theperate wayth?"

"What say you?" Uncle Alistair asked the others still climbing out of the *Wind Cat*. "Felicity?"

"I say we stay together, but without bickering."

Ramses agreed. "Let the truce continue, bicker-free. What say you, Sharrif?"

Sharrif scooped Timsah out of the canal and climbed the bank. "You know more about it than I do."

"I'm thertain we do," the cobra murmured, though only Sharrif heard her finish with a whispered, "thimpleton."

"Very well, the truce continues," Uncle Alistair proclaimed. "Remember, no fangs, no claws."

Ramses chimed in. "And no clubby business from you, Pickelpuss."

The giant scowled and clasped the end of his billy club but did not withdraw it.

Uncle Alistair shielded his eyes and looked up. "We haven't much daylight left. I suggest we spend the night here and head to the Pyramid of Hawara in the morning. It's about twenty-five miles from here. We'll have to go on foot." He glanced at the Countess. "Those without feet may slither. Sharrif, you have matches? Help me build a fire, won't you?"

At differing times, each member of the *Wind Cat* crew regretted the decision to spend the night ashore instead of the boats (which had put some comforting distance between them and Pickelhaube). No one trusted the Countess but they believed she would not act in a treacherous way until they found the gold. Then – oh, yes, *then* they fully expected her to turn on them.

But Pickelhaube? He was a different beast altogether: silent, menacing, powerful, always angry, and (they suspected) explosively violent in an insane, deranged way that might come at any time and for no reason.

After Uncle Alistair, Felicity and Sharrif fell into uneasy sleep and the Countess retired to her basket, Ramses uncurled from the sand and gazed at the giant. "You might as well sleep too, if you ever do," he said. Pickelhaube stared his hard, cold stare but did not react. "Suit yourself," Ramses continued. "But know this, Pickelpuss. You try any funny business, and I'll be on you in a flash."

Ramses sat with his tail wrapped around his paws and his eyes sparkling in the firelight, and he did not turn his steady gaze from the Major until well after the fire had died down and the sun brightened the eastern sky.

4

A twenty-five-mile walk would have made for an extremely long and tiring day but, by lucky chance, an ox cart rumbled toward them before they had gone a half mile from their campsite and took them nearly the entire way to Hawara.

Once again on foot, they passed fields with shoots and stalks and leaves trying mightily to keep their shades of green but losing out to browns and yellows. Dry. Brittle. Crunchy. Withered. Eventually the brown weeds gave way to a barren desert.

They came to a bend and Ramses bounded on ahead. He stopped in the middle of the road and waited for the others to catch up. When they did, he sprang onto Felicity's shoulder and waved his tail back and forth until he found his balance. "And there it is."

"And there is what?" She shielded her eyes. A small dusty mountain rose in the distance. "Something on that hill?"

"It's not a hill," her uncle said. "That, Felicity, is the Pyramid of Hawara."

"*That?*" she asked, astounded. Sharrif did the same: "*That* is a pyramid?"

"One of the later ones, yes," Uncle Alistair explained. "Built not of stone but of mud bricks with a limestone casing, easily removed. After the casing was stolen, nothing could stop the sun and wind and even the occasional rain from attacking what remained. I suggest we make camp at the foot of the pyramid, on what is left of the Labyrinth." He rapped on the side of the wicker basket on Pickelhaube's shoulder. "Almost there, Countess."

Closer, the mound could no longer be mistaken for a mountain for it looked like exactly what it was: the melancholy ruin of a structure made by human hands. It rose over two hundred feet above the desert sands as a heap of thousands upon thousands of crumbling mud bricks. Beside it lay a flat plain dotted with piles of stone chips and low dunes.

When they arrived at its base, Uncle Alistair looked from the pyramid to the canal and back again. He dug the toe of his boot into the sand and it scraped upon stone. "And this is it."

"This is what?" Felicity asked.

He stomped his boot. "This layer of stone reaches from the canal behind us to the base of the pyramid and far into the distance. Bedrock. The floor of the great Egyptian Labyrinth."

Felicity knelt down and pushed away the sand until she, too, reached bedrock. "All this way and all this trouble for this? A floor?"

"Afraid so," her uncle said with a disappointed sigh. He looked at the sky beyond the pyramid. "Sun's nearly gone. Let's set up camp. We can fish in the canal." His shoulders drooped. "Fish again. What wouldn't I give for a steak and mushroom pie about now?"

Writing on back of map:
Faiyum Oasis Map by Sharrif
Ramses spilled tea on it

5

The Countess did not leave her basket until the shadows deepened into solid night lit only by the flickering campfire. Pickelhaube removed the lid and she rose with her usual horrid grin and her monocle shining with reflected firelight. "And here we are, gathered upon the famouth Labyrinth of the Crocodileth." She looked around as if expecting more than a barren plain. "Or rather, it would theem, the great Labyrinth of Nothingneth."

"And now that we *are* here," Ramses said, "the time has come to put our cards on the table. First, the sacred crocodile."

The Countess nodded at Pickelhaube. He reached into his pocket and withdrew the little blue statue. He set it down upon the sand beside Uncle Alistair.

Ramses gazed at it from across the fire. "We know what it says on both back and belly, but we do not yet know what those words mean. Now then, Countess. *The Book of Cobra...*"

"Greatetht book ever penned," she said with pride.

"Which brings up a point," Uncle Alistair said with a puzzled frown. "How, exactly, was it 'penned'? One must, after all, hold a pen in order to pen, and with you and your kind being limbless...quite a feat, if you ask me."

"Which no one did," she observed.

"And what of the phrase Under is Over?" Uncle Alistair asked.

"Under ith Over, yeth," said the cobra with an eager gleam in her eyes.

"Which means what?" Ramses asked.

She blinked twice. "How should I know? I exthpected one of you to tell me. You have all devoted countleth hourth to the thtudy of Egyptology...all exthept that one." She tilted her head in the direction of Sharrif. "The *Book of Cobra* told of an immenthe treasure gathered by the cult of Thobek. Here. In thith very thpot."

"But look around," Uncle Alistair pointed out. "The great Labyrinth of Nothingness, as you said. Nothing at all.."

"We are in the right thpot," the Countess insisted. "I am thertain of it."

Uncle Alistair shrugged. "Suit yourself."

"Thuit mythelf....thuit mythelf. Getting here much thooner would have thuited mythelf quite nithely, but we were delayed...because of *him*." She curled her mouth with distaste and nodded at Sharrif again. "Tell me, Jammpot. Why do you bother with a common, illiterate, camel-boy?"

Sharrif turned to look at her, dumbfounded. Felicity did the same. "What are you thtaring at, you thimpleton?" the Countess asked Sharrif, and she smiled with wicked satisfaction at his downcast eyes and his cheeks turning red with humiliation and shame.

The others sat around the fire, too shocked to move or speak. Sharrif rose to his feet and dashed away from the fire without a word.

"Good riddanthe," the Countess said with a sniff.

Felicity leaped to her feet. She picked up the blue crocodile and would have hurled it at the cobra, but her uncle caught her by the wrist. "The truce," he said in a soft voice. "When it ends you can let her have it, but not now. Go to him. See if you can coax him back."

Felicity backed out of the firelight but did not turn to follow Sharrif until she saw her uncle take off his jacket and roll up his sleeves. "You too," Uncle Alistair said to Ramses.

"I would *ever* so much rather stay and watch," the cat said with an eager grin, but Uncle Alistair would not hear of it. "Pop off now," he said. "Help Felicity find Sharrif."

After Ramses departed (reluctantly), the Countess smirked and said, "Remember, we've called a truthe,"

"Don't you grin at me, you perfectly ridiculous serpent," said Uncle Alistair. "And no, Pickelhaube, no. You stay right there." Pickelhaube turned to the Countess for instructions, but she did not appear to be concerned by Jammpot's anger. If anything, it seemed to please her. "Honethtly, I'll never underthand what you thee in that camel boy. You actually theem to like him."

"Like him?" Uncle Alstair repeated. "Heavens no."

"Thought not."

"I don't like him. I *love* him, as I would my very own nephew, if I had one."

"Love him! A common, thimple-minded..."

"Don't start with that again, you illiterate cobra," Uncle Alistair said.

"Illiterate!" the serpent returned, outraged.

"You couldn't translate a hieroglyph if your miserable life depended on it." She opened her mouth to say something, but Uncle Alistair stopped her: "Oh, I could wring your slithery neck. I truly could. Building yourself up by tearing down a boy. Shameful. And why? To make yourself look good, which is a monumental task if *ever* there was one. To prop yourself up as something more than the common, black-hearted, illiterate fool of a cobra that you are."

"Common? *Me?*"

"Common as dirt. Blowing out someone else's lantern, as if that will make yours burn all the brighter."

The Countess blinked. "What lantern?"

"Oh, do be quiet. You, who came by your false title by way of a bite to Count Frederick Schnitzel von Hyss. Really should have checked his luggage, poor chap. Let us have an end to this adventure. Either we find the treasure, or we do not. Either way, I shall look forward to seeing the last of your hairnet and monocle and your ghastly grin, not to mention that wordless gargoyle of a manservant who does not appear to realize the Great War is over." He turned to Pickelhaube. "You lost, by the way."

The Countess tried again to say something, but Uncle Alistair wouldn't hear of it. On and on he went, letting her know exactly what he thought of her. When finished, he folded his arms across his chest and said: "And there you have it."

She had abandoned her smirk for something the professor had never seen in her before. It might have been cold fury. It might have been shame. He could not tell. She slithered into her basket where she coiled over herself as she settled in. "We will thpeak more of this in the morning. Hermann-Düüfuth. My lid."

The giant rose from the sand and Uncle Alistair scoffed at his ferocious scowl. "I suppose I must have it out with you too, you great galumphing gargoyle. Very well. If it's a brawl you want, it's a brawl you shall have."

Major Pickelhaube did not take up the offer.

He dropped the lid onto the wicker basket. Instead of attacking Jammpot or returning to his place, he withdrew two wires from his pocket.

Uncle Alistair watched, puzzled, as he slipped the wires into the wicker and gave them a twist to secure the lid to the base. Why would he do such a thing? Afraid the wind might blow it off?

The answer came a moment later when Pickelhaube lifted the basket into his mighty arms. A voice inside asked, "Why do you dithturb my thlumber?"

Without pause, the giant strode to the bank and threw it. The basket landed halfway down and tumbled over twice before landing in the canal with a splash.

Uncle Alistair leaped to his feet with a gasp. "Good God! Pickelhaube! What *can* you be thinking!?"

The water was not as deep as usual, but enough remained to rush through the wicker and drag the basket down, lower and lower until it disappeared with a gulp. Bubbles hissed on the surface and brought with them the sound of an underwater scream.

"Countess!" Uncle Alistair cried. Down the bank he went and plowed into the water. He felt around, frantic. "Countess!"

There! He jammed his fingers into the wicker and lifted. Water poured from the basket as he carried it to the bank, surprised by how heavy it was. He dropped it and pulled on the lid.

The wires held but the wicker tore under his grip and up she came through the gash he made, coughing and blinking and slick with canal water.

Her hairnet had slipped down over her entire head and her lace neckband had sprung loose. Her monocle lay tight against her eye, held there by the hairnet hood. "What?" she gasped. "How?"

Her tongue slid through the hairnet and nearly touched Uncle Alistair's face as he continued to tear at the lid. He moved his head to avoid it, but out it came – *quiver, quiver, quiver* – and slipped back in again. "I say, Countess…that thing with your tongue…might you pause for a moment?"

"Thith?" – *quiver, quiver, quiver.*

"If you don't mind. Most unsettling."

"What happened?" she asked in a voice muffled by the hairnet still covering her mouth.

"Him." Uncle Alistair nodded at the top of the bank. "Let me help you with that."

"Hermann-Düüfuth?" she asked, genuinely shocked.

"Haven't a clue why." He lifted the hairnet from her face and arranged it on her head. "Can't quite…without hair…can't quite figure out how to…there then. Good enough."

"Hermann-Düüfuth did thith?" she asked with a glimmer of hurt in her eyes. "To *me*?"

"Wholly unexpected."

"And you thaved me."

"Even more unexpected, truly," said Uncle Alistair. "But one cannot simply allow someone to drown, can one? Even someone like you, so unlikeable and, frankly, hideous."

"But…*why* would he do it?" Her shock and hurt faded into a much more forceful look of rage. "Traitor!" she spat out, and she poured from the basket and slithered up the bank. Uncle Alistair followed, scrambling up on all fours. When he reached the top, he nearly fell on top of her.

She had stopped dead.

He did the same, frozen in place by the sight of Pickelhaube flanked by the entire crew of river pirates.

Umbalali lay beside him in full tribal war paint and ceremonial headdress of red feathers, and a gleam of evil triumph in his eyes.

"Thcoundrel!" the Countess spat out, glaring at her unfaithful manservant. "You tried to athathinate me!" She started toward him, but the pirates slithered forward to stop her. One of the jackals snapped at her.

Umbalali sent a shudder of warning down the length of his muscular body. "You came for the gold without me," he snarled. "*My* gold." His belly scales glimmered in the firelight. "Major Pickelhaube and I shall take over from now on, cobra. Now where is it?"

"How many timeth do I have to tell you, python?" the cobra sneered, and her neck hood expanded. "I do not yet know."

"I do not ask for the gold and jewels," said Umbalali. "I ask for the key to find them. I ask for the blue crocodile."

Pickelhaube looked down at the place where he set the little crocodile and he took a sudden deep intake of breath, shocked to see only marks in the sand. His eyes shot up, looking out to the dark, looking out toward the pyramid.

Labyrinth of the Crocodiles

That girl! She had it. She was holding it. She threatened to throw it at the Countess before she and the cat ran off to comfort the boy.

Umbalali followed his gaze and knew at once what they had to do. "Come Major," he said. "The rest of you keep watch over them." The pirates hissed and growled and spread out to surround Uncle Alistair and the Countess. "If they make a move, bite and strike and kill them both."

6

"I see Sharrif," Ramses said from atop Felicity's shoulder.

The lantern rocked back and forth in her hand and sent shadows over the limestone blocks scattered here and there. The crumbling pyramid rose before her, but even that was nearly hidden by the night's shadows.

Ramses could see everything, of course. He saw Sharrif, even with his black robe and black hair. He saw him change direction after Sharrif noticed Felicity's lantern trailing after him, and he saw him run toward the pyramid where he hid behind one of the blocks. "Up ahead," Ramses said.

When Felicity rounded the corner of the block, she found Sharrif seated against the limestone with his arms around his knees and Timsah beside him with his eyes glistening in the lanternlight.

"Why would you do that?" Felicity asked, out of breath. "Why would you listen to a single thing that cobra says? Why would you run from *her!*"

"I'm not finished running."

Felicity looked around at the featureless desert but saw only blocks, only sand, only darkness. "Running where?"

"I can reach Cairo in a few days," Sharrif said. "From there, I'll get a boat north to the monastery."

169

"But why? Because of what the Countess said?"

Sharrif dropped his hands and set his back against the block. "I'm not one of you."

"You don't have to be one of us," Felicity said. "Back in the Flamingo and Lime I told Ramses I wanted you to like the same things I like." She dropped to her knees beside him. "I thought everyone should like the same things I like, but I was wrong."

"I can't be like you," Sharrif said.

"You can be anything you want."

"I cleaned the camel stables at the monastery. When you came, I thought I could be something more...but, no. I'm a stable boy."

Felicity stared, confused. "That was your work. It's what you did. It's not who you *are*."

"I can't read!" he shouted. "I was left on a doorstep. I'm not one of you. My father wasn't a pilot and my mother wasn't a lady. My parents left me on a doorstep dressed in rags. I can't be like you."

Felicity was shocked. It never occurred to her that he would take her words to mean something so entirely different. She only meant he didn't have to share the same interests – not that he was in any way apart from her or beneath her as a person. She would never think that about him. It would never occur to her to think it! He could not see the tears that sprang quietly to her eyes. This boy she thought of as a brother, the only brother she would ever have, who had shared adventures and dangers since the day they met – *this* was how he saw their friendship all this time? That she thought of him as somehow below and apart and different? "You believe I would think that about you?" she asked.

Sharrif didn't answer. Ramses circled around Felicity and sat between them. "And what do you think of me, Felicity?"

"You?" she asked the cat, confused. "What do I think of you?"

170

"Are we friends?" Ramses asked.

"We've always been friends."

"Dear friends?"

"The dearest." She looked at Sharrif. "One of the dearest."

"You might even admire me?" Ramses asked.

"You know I do."

"Why?"

"Because you're clever," she returned, even as she wondered why the conversation had drifted away from Sharrif. "You know things. You get me out of trouble. You get us all out of trouble."

Ramses padded over to Sharrif and set one paw on his foot. "Did you hear?" The boy didn't answer. "Did you?"

"Yes. So?"

"So I am an Egyptian, the same as you. I was abandoned, the same as you."

Sharrif shook his head. "Not the same."

"Not exactly the same, you're right," Ramses said. "I'm not an orphan for I know my father. He's a thief and a scoundrel, but my father all the same. You do not know for sure if you're an orphan. Felicity is, but you have no proof you are."

"I was left on a doorstep."

"And I was found by her uncle between the front paws of the Great Sphinx, abandoned, alone and swarming with fleas. If we must compete over who had the worst beginnings, I win."

"But you're Ramses Faro!" Sharrif exclaimed. "You write books! You're famous. You can read."

"So can you," Ramses said.

"Not very well."

"Well enough."

"But you *know* things," Sharrif exclaimed.

Felicity had heard enough. She set the lantern and blue crocodile down and grabbed Sharrif by the shoulders. "You know things too!" she insisted. "When you said you weren't one of us, I thought you meant you weren't an Egyptologist. I had no idea you meant you weren't one of *us*. Me and Ramses and Uncle Alistair. You *are* one of us, Sharrif. You'll always be one of us. We want you with us always. You know things we couldn't learn in a hundred thousand years."

"You can read hieroglyphs," Sharrif said.

"And you can read the river!" Felicity exclaimed. "You can read boats and camels and deserts. You don't know what the writing in a tomb means? Who cares? Ramses and I do. But we would have an awful time getting to that tomb if you weren't there to show us the way."

Sharrif looked her in the eye, even though the light was behind her and hid her face. "You don't think I'm stupid?"

"Oh Sharrif!" Felicity threw her arms around him. "Never! I would never – I *could* never think that about you. Never, never, never!"

When she released him, Ramses tapped Sharrif's foot again with his paw. "The more important question is this. Do *you* think it?"

Sharrif hesitated. He released his knees and stroked Timsah along his back.

Ramses stood before him and would not release him from his gaze. "You will never have trouble finding someone to point out all the things you cannot do," he said.

Sharrif tried to turn away but found he couldn't. The cat did not move. "The greater battle," Ramses said, "comes when the one pointing out the things you cannot do – is you. Understand?"

Sharrif nodded, but without much enthusiasm. "Careful, don't squish Timsah," he said when Felicity grabbed him by the shoulders again. The crocodile crawled onto the boy's lap.

"I don't care if you can't tell Amenemhat III from Aunt Ludmilla-Florence, or a pepper from a peeper," Felicity said. "I don't care about anything you can't do because I know what you *can* do. You can be a brother to me, and a friend, and as smart and clever as this very smart and very clever cat."

The smart and clever cat suddenly tensed. His ears shot up and swiveled. He stared at a dim glow on a nearby block, growing brighter. "Lower the lantern."

"Why?" asked Sharrif.

"Someone's coming."

Felicity turned a knob. The lantern dimmed to a tiny spot of flame. "What do you see?"

"Not quite sure, be back in a jiff," Ramses said, and he darted off before she could ask anything more.

"Who do you think it is?" Sharrif asked.

"Uncle Alistair," Felicity said. "Looking for us."

"How long is a jiff?"

"Probably longer than a flash, but not as long as a smidge."

Sharrif laughed. Felicity did too, but her laugh quickly faded. "You're not going to run off to the monastery?"

"I don't..." Sharrif hesitated. "I don't really sort of think I want to go." He focused on the shadows of her face where he knew her eyes would be. "I guess you don't think I should go either."

"I can't think of anything worse," Felicity said.

He smiled but neither one could see the expression of the other. Even so, she sensed his smile and she threw her arms around him again. "Sorry Timsah," she said, and the little crocodile chirped happily as they embraced.

Looking over her shoulder, Sharrif saw a small black shadow dashing over the sand. "Ramses," he said, and she released him and turned in time to meet him.

"They're coming," Ramses said. "Hide the lantern."

"Blow it out," Sharrif said. "I have matches."

"Who's coming?" Felicity asked and — *puff* — she blew out the lantern. "Uncle Alistair?"

"Pickelpuss." Ramses peeped around the side of the limestone block. "And Umbalali."

"Umbalali *here?*" Sharrif said with a gasp, and Timsah softly chirped in his arms. "Run," the little croc said, "Run. Snap, crunch, *run!*"

"Quiet, now." Ramses studied the scattered blocks, the sand, the desert. "Come."

They left the shelter of the limestone block and found themselves in a far worse, far more exposed position.

On the left lay the empty floor of the Labyrinth.

On the right, a wide plain of flat and empty desert.

They had nowhere to hide in either direction.

Sharrif's heart pounded so hard he worried the python might hear it. "Now what?"

"This way," Ramses said, and he led them away from Pickelhaube and Umbalali to the base of the pyramid. "Only one way left for us," he whispered. "We have no choice."

"Up there?" Felicity asked, gazing at the crumbling ruin towering high and black above them.

"Not up," Ramses said. "In!"

With that, he led them onto a downward sloping path toward a slit in the rock, menacing, black and gaping, and nearly hidden in the limestone wall.

Felicity stopped on the path with her heart in her throat. "In there?" she asked.

"We have no choice," Ramses said again, urging her on. "Come, now. Hurry!"

"What is this?" Sharrif asked, his voice trembling.

"A portal," he returned, and with that, he led them into the secret entrance to the Pyramid of Hawara discovered nearly forty years before by Uncle Alistair's friend, Sir William Flinders-Petrie.

Ramses Faro

VII. Under Is Over

Ramses Faro

1

Sharrif relit the lantern. He kept the flame so low they could barely see the walls of grey stone. The tunnel was grim and tight and as cold as a tomb. They stayed close to the entrance, hoping Pickelhaube and Umbalali would pass them by.

But no. The python's high trilling war cry quivered its way into the tunnel.

"Our tracks," Felicity whispered.

"Our scent too," Ramses said. He imagined the python's tongue tasting the air, searching for traces of his prey, searching especially for Sharrif. "We have to go in. Deeper."

Sharrif held Timsah close against his chest. "How far?"

Ramses stared into the pitch-black tunnel. "As far as we can."

Thirty feet in, the floor went from stone to dried mud.

The ceiling became so low they bent over to avoid scraping it with their heads. With the already narrow walls on each side, it felt like they were making their way into the smaller end of a funnel lying on its side. They moved forward in a crouch, and soon dropped to their knees. Before them, the tunnel pinched down to a narrow slit. "How far can we go?" Felicity asked.

"As far as we can," Ramses said again. He looked behind her. A light approached the entrance from outside. "Don't stop."

He slunk into the blackness of the narrow slit. As light as he was, his paws sank into the putrid mud. Sharrif's dim lantern showed him a way ahead – but to where? "Looks impossible, but it's not," he told the others. "Come."

Felicity nodded and swallowed hard, and they followed him on their hands and knees.

He told them to imagine a drainage pipe sloping down and curving up again. Water from the canal long ago filled the bottom of the curve, along with centuries of mud.

"How can water and mud get inside a pyramid?" Felicity whispered.

"My guess is that canal was built long after," Sharrif said. "This place is probably full of water all the time. If it wasn't for the drought we would never get through here."

"Are you sure we can now?" Felicity asked, her voice filled with doubt. Sharrif lifted the lantern. Twelve inches remained between the mud floor and stone ceiling.

"Timsah, come ahead with me,' Ramses said. "You two will need to pull or push yourselves through, whatever does the trick." He looked back at the entrance again. Its edges glowed with approaching light. "Now," he said. "Go."

Felicity kicked off her shoes and Sharrif slid out of his sandals. "Desperate times…" she said.

They lay upon their stomachs and slid along the oozing mud, pushed by fingers and toes. Sharrif shoved the lantern ahead before each slide. Ramses and Timsah gingerly stepped upon the slime before them, heading into utter darkness.

The slit narrowed even further. Felicity felt the stone ceiling brush the back of her head while her chin slid along only a half inch from the filthy mud. "How much further?" When she opened her mouth to speak, the bottom of her chin dipped into the clammy ooze

"Not far," Ramses said somewhere up ahead. "Keep going. Almost through."

The corridor began an upward tilt. The space between mud and ceiling increased. Eventually the mud disappeared altogether, and they were once again in a dry tunnel of cut stone, and now the walls widened into a corridor.

Again, Ramses looked behind, alerted by a low sound of metal scraping against stone. The glow of Pickelhaube's lantern seeped through the narrow slit. Sharrif saw it too. "Can *he* get through there?"

"We shall see," Ramses said. He crept back toward the narrow slit. There he saw the giant squeezed into the tunnel, plowing through the mud with his hands curled into claws to drag himself forward and the point of his helmet scraping against the rock above. He imagined the python slithering behind him with his horrid tongue darting in and out.

Ramses' fur bristled and he rushed back to the others. "On we go."

"On we go to where?" Sharrif asked and he lifted the lantern. Rubble and broken rocks littered the floor. Beyond the rubble, a solid wall marked the end of the passageway. They saw no doors or exits on either side.

"Dead end," Felicity whispered.

Ramses ran ahead and inspected the solid walls. "Only looks like a dead end," he said. "It's a false portal." He looked up. Nothing there either. He returned to Felicity and Sharrif without taking his eyes from the ceiling. "Ah, there! Behind you. Look up."

They saw a small hole in the ceiling, wide enough for a man to crawl through. "A trap door, broken by thieves long ago," Ramses explained. "We need to get up there."

The glow from the narrow slit brightened behind them. "Quickly!" Ramses said. He clambered up Sharrif and sprang from his shoulder up into the hole.

Lamplight from below showed him a second passageway with walls as blank as the first. It also showed him a rope ladder lying in a heap upon the floor, anchored by a limestone block. The unburned end of a candle lay beside it, covered with dust. He pushed the ladder to the edge of the hole with his snout and over it went. "Left by Sir William," he called down to Felicity and Sharrif. "Hasn't been used these last forty years."

Felicity tugged the ladder a couple of times to see if it would hold her weight and she stepped upon the first rung. It snapped beneath her foot.

"Try again," Ramses said. "Hurry"

She stepped onto the next rung. Firm. Sharrif held the ladder steady while she climbed to the higher passageway. "You next," she said.

"Timsah first." Sharrif tossed the little crocodile and Felicity caught him. Next went the lantern, and last came Sharrif, climbing the fragile ladder. He reached the top and pulled it up behind. "Pickelpuss can't climb that without breaking it, but better to hide our trail."

"Good thinking, but it won't stop him," Ramses said. "That brute is so tall he can haul himself up without a ladder."

182

He pawed at the dusty candle. "We'll take this with us. And we can turn the lamp up now. Full."

Before them lay a corridor like the one below but heading in a different direction, with no paintings or carvings upon the walls, only blank stone.

After several more false portals and trapdoors and new corridors, they came to a room with a floor made of a single gigantic rock. "This is the stone lowered onto the burial chamber," Ramses said. "They expected it would protect the pharaoh." He approached a hole at the edge of the rock. "But it takes more than a hundred-ton stone to stop a determined thief. They tunneled down beside it."

"To where?" Sharrif asked.

"Straight down into the pharaoh's burial chamber." He crouched at the edge of the hole. "I see part of a ladder. Useless. The ropes have rotted completely away. I see water too. Oh, that canal. It's ruined everything. Pity."

"How deep?" Felicity asked.

Sharrif dropped a stone chip over the edge. *Plop*. Ramses tilted his head. "Again." He swiveled his ears. *Plop*, followed by a clack only he could hear. "Too deep for me."

Behind them came a bang and a scrape, and a hollow echo of a footstep.

"They're coming," Felicity said, peering into the darkness.

Without warning, Timsah waddled to the hole and jumped. Sharrif tried to catch him – "Timsah!" – but too late. The crocodile dropped through the tunnel and plunged into the water.

"Crunch," Timsah called to the others when he rose to the surface.

Ramses asked: "By crunch you mean…what? Too deep for me?"

chirp

"Too deep for Felicity and Sharrif?" the cat asked.

croak

"Which means I shall ride upon one of you," Ramses said to the others. "Who first?"

Felicity looked over the edge. "Once we go down there..."

Ramses finished the thought. "How will we get back out?" Felicity nodded and he said, "Not quite sure about that yet." His left ear twitched at the sound of an echo from behind.

"What if we *can't* get out?" Felicity asked. "Even if we escape from Pickelhaube and that python, how would Uncle Alistair find us? He doesn't know we're in here."

Another echo sounded. A rock shifted and clacked in a distant passageway. This time they all heard it.

Ramses looked from the hole to the corridor. She was right. It was entirely possible there was no way out. At the same time, there was no way out of their current predicament, but for the drop into the burial chamber below, and Pickelhaube and Umbalali were on their way. "This," he said, "is one of the pickeliest of all pickles we've ever been in. Truly."

Sharrif sat and draped his legs over the edge. "I hate that snake," he said, and that settled it. He spun around and lowered himself with his hands still upon the floor, clinging to the edge...and he let go.

The drop was not nearly as high as the one at the Nilometer and he did not reinjure his foot when he landed in a crouch in the knee-deep water. Timsah paddled up to him, chirping. "I'm fine," he said and patted him on the head. "Drop the lantern," he called up to Felicity.

After he caught it, Felicity dropped into the chamber in the same way. Ramses came last. Felicity caught him and set him on her shoulder. "Magnificent," he whispered.

"What is?" Felicity asked. She saw only gloom and shadows in the dim light.

"Turn up the lantern," he replied.

Sharrif turned up the flame, and they gaped with eyes wide and their breath caught in their chests, stunned by the majesty of the burial chamber of Amenemhat III, Pharaoh of the Twelfth Dynasty of the Middle Kingdom. The invading canal water had damaged the lower third of the walls and were mud-colored and stripped of paint. But above the damage...

Color!

The chamber shimmered with spectacular paintings of the pharaoh and his royal court and a treasury of sacred symbols, all in dazzling golds and reds and blues, with snow-white robes, eyes black and piercing, vibrant green leaves and colorful birds and flowers.

Ramses tapped on Felicity's arm to draw her attention to a massive stone sarcophagus in the center of the room. Its heavy lid lay on its side on the floor, propped against it.

"Is his mummy in there?" she asked, but a quick look showed only fragments of bone and charcoal inside.

"Thieves again," Ramses said. "There was a wooden coffin embedded with jewels. They didn't bother to pry them out, simply burned the entire thing. His mummy too, for the jewels sewn into his linens. Imagine that...once the most powerful man in all the world." He tensed when another echo sounded, closer. "Show me the blue crocodile's belly again."

Sharrif set the candle upon a stone altar built against a wall. Felicity placed the crocodile beside it, turned onto its back. Ramses hopped onto the altar. Crouching before the crocodile, he pushed up his spectacles and squinted at the tiny hieroglyphs. "I'll keep looking for something new – or rather, *trying* to find something new," he said, frustrated by the thought. "You do the same."

Sharrif and Felicity waded through the burial chamber and studied the walls and ceiling. Timsah followed Sharrif so closely that he bumped against his legs every few seconds.

Another echo came, this one louder than the others.

"Keep looking," Ramses said without taking his eyes off the crocodile.

"I don't know what to look for," Sharrif whispered to Felicity. He ran his fingers over a series of ridges on the wall. "It's all pictures to me. A baboon over there. Some birds over here. And these things...plants of some kind. Maybe reeds."

Felicity's eyes snapped to the wall where he stood.

Reeds!

She splashed over and ran both hands over the reeds, painted green and gold within a series of straight vertical grooves upon the wall. "Sleeps in the reeds..." She crouched and felt the wall beneath the water. "Here!"

Ramses looked up from the crocodile's belly.

"The Sacred Crocodile Sleeps in the Reeds," Felicity said. "It wasn't the sarcophagus from Kom Ombo after all. *These* are the reeds! Down here...an indent carved into the wall."

"Shaped like a crocodile?" Ramses asked, his eyes widening behind his spectacles.

"The same shape and size as our blue one."

Ramses looked down at the blue crocodile. "The key." He tapped it with his paw. Sharrif brought it to Felicity and held the lantern while she pressed the crocodile against the indent. "It fits." She pushed it into the wall.

Nothing happened.

"Now what?" Sharrif asked.

Felicity shrugged. Ramses sat beside the candle. His ears swiveled. He heard something...*almost* heard something.

Dust drifted from the ceiling. Something rumbled, stone against stone, grinding. Two lines cracked up the wall behind him. He sprang to the edge of the sarcophagus and used his tail to balance on the edge.

The altar began to sink. Flecks of stone rattled into the water. Ramses leapt to Sharrif's shoulder and they shielded their eyes against the rolling dust. When it cleared, they gazed in silent wonder at a gap in the wall where the altar stood, two feet high and one foot wide.

It stopped two inches below the surface of the water, which now flowed through the gap and splashed into darkness beyond. Ramses peered into the yawning hole. "A staircase. Leading down."

The water from the burial chamber cascaded down the stairs and turned the ancient dust to slick mud. "Down to where?" Felicity asked.

"No idea. No one now alive has ever seen this." Another clack and echo sounded from above, closer than ever. "Quickly now," Ramses said. "Squeeze through this gap. Take the blue crocodile. It may hold more answers."

After they climbed through, he glanced up at the hole in the ceiling. Its edges suddenly glowed with light and his fur bristled at the sight of Umbalali's head oozing down into the chamber with the handle of a lantern gripped in his jaws. "Hurry!" he whispered, and he jumped through the hole, following his friends.

2

Down they went, climbing down the hidden staircase to a place far below the pyramid. They'd left their shoes and sandals far behind in the narrow tunnel and mud now squished between their toes. The walls dripped with moisture. An echo of a splash washed over them from behind.

"They've reached the burial chamber," Ramses said. "That gap in the wall will stop them until Pickelpuss breaks the edges to fit through." He hopped down the stairs before them, his paws and legs slick with mud. "I see the bottom. Save the candle for later."

Sharrif blew out the candle and dropped it into his pocket. He had to push it past Timsah who nestled inside with his front paws over the edge like a joey kangaroo in its mother's pouch. Sharrif patted him on the head before pulling his hand out again. "Good boy."

When they reached the bottom, Felicity lifted the lantern, and they paused - staggered by the sight of an army of crocodile mummies lining both sides of a dusty cobblestone lane like sentries guarding a long-forgotten road. Each one lay with the tip of its tail against the wall behind and its snout facing the snout of the crocodile on the opposite side.

"What *is* this place?" Felicity asked, her voice a blend of fear and wonder.

"A necropolis*," Ramses said. "A city of the dead. These must have been the crocodiles who lived in the temple, the sons of Sobek worshipped by the priests."

Sharrif snapped his fingers. "I know where we are! That book you were reading on the boat...oh, weeks ago now." He stopped speaking, startled by a clacking noise behind. They turned in time to see a stone clatter down from the staircase and thud against one of the mummies.

"Pickelpuss is breaking through," Ramses whispered, and Sharrif picked up where he left off. "That book," he said. "You told me to pay attention, even though I didn't want to. It said there was a road that connected the pyramid to the Labyrinth."

Felicity tapped her foot on a dusty cobblestone. "Wouldn't a road be on the land above?"

"No, the book said an underground road. Remember? I said I thought that was strange."

Ramses suddenly gasped and hopped onto Felicity's shoulder, startling her. "What is it?" she asked with her hand over her heart.

"What you just said, Sharrif." He peered at him. "No one would build a road underground. Unless..." Another rock tumbled down the staircase behind. "We mustn't linger," he said, and Felicity started down the road between the mummies with Ramses upon her shoulder. "Unless what?" she asked.

"Under is Over," Ramses said. "I know what it means. The Labyrinth wasn't destroyed by the Romans."

"But we saw it," Sharrif said, catching up to them. "That huge slab of bedrock in front of the pyramid. You said it was a floor. So did Uncle Alistair."

"We were wrong." Ramses gazed beyond the crocodile mummies trailing into the gloom. "The Labyrinth is still here. It's *under* that massive rock."

"But how?" Felicity asked, confused.

Sharrif's eyes widened. "Because that rock isn't a floor," he said, and he looked up into the darkness above, stunned by the thought. "It's a roof!"

3

They walked down the sloping lane in their tight circle of lantern light. Two colossal statues of the god Sobek loomed out of the darkness, one on each side of the road and each with the muscular, bare-chested body of a man and the head of a Nile crocodile, staring, threatening, as if to say, "Pass at your own peril!" A single block of stone connected the tops of the sentinels to form a gateway leading into a realm of shadow.

Ramses whispered the remembered words from the belly of the blue crocodile: "Terrible is the name of the gate-keeper. Sobek is the name of the gate-keeper." Beyond the terrible gate, a range of pillars stretched into a vast silence.

They might have paused a little longer before stepping into the Labyrinth, but another rock tumbled down the staircase behind them.

"He's coming," Sharrif said.

They approached the Sobek Gate one slow step at a time and crossed over the threshold. As soon as they did, a rumble as loud as a freight train roared over them. The floor trembled. Dust billowed down.

Felicity and Sharrif froze in place, terrified, but Ramses jumped down from Felicity's shoulder and urged them on. "Pass through!" he called over the roar.

The moment they stepped over the threshold, the sound echoed off into unknown hallways, and silence closed over them once more.

"What *was* that?" Felicity asked.

"Thunder machines," Ramses said. "Designed to scare intruders."

"Well done," Felicity said, looking up at the gate.

Their lantern showed a bewildering forest of stone before them, with columns and pillars and statues in every direction. A thin coating of dried mud rose to a height of four feet on each structure to mark the usual height of the invading canal water. Above the mud, the walls and columns dazzled with paintings like those in the burial chamber (though a few columns remained unpainted and stood like dead trees in a colorful forest).

Sharrif looked back over his shoulder. "Once we go in, we'll never find our way back."

Ramses sat upon the cobblestones and wrapped his tail around his paws. "We're not going to try," he said. "Even without Pickelpuss following, we cannot climb out of the burial chamber. We can only go forward, though we do not know if the way forward has a way out."

"Doesn't that mean we're trapped?" Sharrif asked.

"Possibly," Ramses returned.

The boy looked at Felicity. She looked back at him, and they both looked at Ramses. "You don't seem very scared," she said.

"I'm not."

"I am," Felicity said.

"I am too," Sharrif admitted, and a tiny, chirped *am too* came from inside his pocket.

Ramses looked up at the ceiling, but it was too high and dark, even for his eyes. "I'm not scared, because I've decided not to be scared. What is the worst that could happen? I mean the truly horribly worst?"

"We could die down here," Felicity said.

"Do we know for certain that's going to happen?"

"No," she admitted. "Not for certain."

"Which means we still have hope," Ramses said, "which means the truly horribly worst is not within sight." He padded up to her and rubbed against her ankle. "Being afraid of things that might happen is often a way to make sure they *do* happen. Now then...we need a guide, and I believe we've found one. Remember...all the way back in Kom Ombo. On the wall, the cartouche of the pharaoh's name..."

"Amun is in front," Sharrif said, surprised he remembered. "Amenemhat's name. Right?"

Ramses nodded. "His birth name," he said, and he again recited a part of the incantation upon the crocodile's belly: "The secret is opened for those who follow the birth of the King."

"Which means what?" Felicity asked.

"It means we pay no attention to the statues of the king, of Amenemhat III himself. We pay attention to his *name*. Amun is in front. Be on the lookout for him."

"How?" Sharrif asked. "These gods and pharaohs all look the same to me."

"Yes, when Amun comes as a man. But remember the Temple of Karnak. When he doesn't come as a man, he comes in another shape." Ramses strode toward a sphinx with the body of a lion and the head of a ram. "And here he is, gazing in the direction we need to follow."

4

They wandered the Labyrinth in silence, passing this way and that, through doors and chambers and hallways. Each time they came upon a sphinx with a ram's head, they changed direction onto a path shown to them by Amun, and it wasn't long before they all realized they were hopelessly lost. Even Ramses had no idea if they were moving forward or backward or going in circles. Sharrif lit his candle again to give them a little more light.

A deep rumble washed over them from behind.

"Pickelpuss passed through the thunder gate," Ramses said. "No time to dawdle."

More passageways and more chambers with multiple openings leading to more passageways, more gateways and portals. Everything had an unsettling quality of being exactly like all they had seen before. The only things that did not appear similar were the few unpainted columns, though they were the only things that truly *were* exactly alike.

After stepping through another doorway, they heard a sudden squeak from Sharrif's pocket, and an urgent *chirp chirp run chirp run.*

"What's the matter?" Sharrif asked, but Timsah squirmed out of his pocket without answering and dashed into the darkness. Sharrif started after him but feared the sudden rush of air might blow out his candle again. He set it on the floor and ran after his friend.

He found him curled up against a pillar. "What's the matter?" He squatted down beside him and stroked his snout with his forefinger. "What happened?"

Felicity and Ramses came up from behind. "Maybe that thunder sound scared him," Felicity suggested.

"Did you see something?" Sharrif asked. Before Timsah could answer, Felicity's hand shot out and clamped upon his shoulder. Her grip was so strong Sharrif knew immediately what it meant: *Don't say anything. Don't move.*

He slowly turned to look at her. Wide-eyed and pale, she stood gazing back toward the way they had come. Sharrif turned further and saw the fur rise on Ramses' back and his ears drop flat upon his head. He, too, was looking back at the way they had come.

Sharrif swallowed hard and turned further.

His candle burned in the distance as a pinpoint of flame in a vast plain of darkness.

Something lay beside it, barely visible in the candlelight.

"Hide the lantern," Ramses whispered.

Sharrif folded his robe over it while turning down the flame. "What is that?"

"Crocodile," the cat said.

Sharrif stared. It was one of the mummies, thick and black and still. "But how?" he whispered. "It wasn't there before." No one answered. "Should I get that candle?"

Far in the distance, they caught a glimpse of another light but only for a second before it passed behind an unseen wall or column.

"Leave it," Ramses said.

"But they'll see it," Sharrif said. "They'll know where we are." He started toward the candle but stopped dead when the crocodile's mouth crackled open. The ancient linen around its jaws tore into dusty threads. The candle's flame glistened on the black teeth and the mummified tongue dried into black leather.

The distant light came again, this time close enough to make out the figure holding it.

"Pickelpuss," Ramses said.

The crocodile mummy shifted. It dragged its heavy body closer to the candlelight. They shivered with horror when it hissed a dry, rattling hiss. It shut its jaws with a crack and spun around. Its tail snuffed out the candle and sent it tumbling away into darkness.

"Leave it," Ramses whispered. "We must go. Quickly."

Sharrif lifted his robe from the lantern and turned up the flame. When he did, he noticed something on the floor beside Felicity. "What's this?" He picked it up but immediately dropped it again and wiped his fingers on his robe.

"What is it?" she asked.

He could barely form the words when he replied in a hoarse whisper: "A red feather."

He looked up and his blood went cold. Umbalali was *right there!* Behind Felicity with his head seven feet from the floor, peering down at her with his mouth wide open and his face streaked with war paint.

Felicity did not know what hit her. The python's jaws clamped around the back of her neck. His thick body shuffled forward, curling and twining to pull her into his coils.

Sharrif couldn't move. He couldn't think. He didn't know what to do.

Timsah darted in and snapped at the python, though his tiny jaws couldn't get a grip.

Ramses, meanwhile, had sprung into action in a split-second. Up he went as if he had springs on his feet. When he came down, he unsheathed his claws.

The snake hissed. He opened his jaws and released Felicity, though he threw another coil around her body to keep her close. He snapped at Ramses, trying to crush him with a bite, but the cat was too fast.

Down! Up! Slash!

Umbalali could not catch him. The cat was a whirling dervish, slashing until the python felt the shadows themselves were attacking him.

He pulled Felicity closer, tighter, squeezing. The blue crocodile toppled from her pocket.

Her face turned red. Each time she released a breath, the snake tightened his grip. She stared at Sharrif with panicked eyes, urging him to run away.

Umbalali squeezed again. Ramses continued his attack. Timsah did the same.

Sharrif looked around, frantic, searching for a weapon.

Without thinking, he grabbed the blue crocodile. He clasped its tail in both hands and drew back. "Ramses!" he called, and the cat gave the snake a final slash upon the snout before leaping away.

Sharrif swung with all his might. The blue crocodile caught Umbalali on the side of the head. *Crack!* The feathered headdress flew like a panicked bird. The blue crocodile broke in half. Sharrif held the tail end and drew back again, but before he could strike, the python shook his head and with a groaning hiss, he collapsed. His jaw struck the floor and his coils relaxed into a heap.

Sharrif grabbed Felicity's arm. She slid from the snake's grip, gasping for breath. She pointed at the broken blue crocodile on the floor. Sharrif picked it up and held the two pieces together, as if that might somehow make it whole again.

Umbalali moved beside him. He opened his milky-blue eyes and caught them in a glare of rage.

Sharrif helped Felicity to her feet. He handed her the broken crocodile. "Can you run?"

"I will, even if I can't," she said through her gasping breath.

A new light appeared behind them. Heavy footsteps pounded the floor, approaching.

"Go," Ramses said. "Follow the rams. I'll catch up. Hurry!"

Sharrif grabbed Timsah and he raced into the corridor with Felicity behind. Ramses crept away from Umbalali and huddled close against the base of a ram sphinx. Pickelhaube appeared. He saw Umbalali stretched out upon the floor. He held the lantern over him. He pulled his club from his belt and lifted it.

"Why?" Ramses wondered.

The question remained unanswered. Before the giant could bring the club down upon the snake, there came a roar from the shadows and the crocodile mummy rumbled toward the giant with its jaws open and linens trailing behind.

Ramses nearly cheered at the sight, but his joy turned to shock when the giant turned to confront his attacker.

He didn't hesitate. He didn't run. Striding forward, he brought his club down with a crash upon the mummy. Dust exploded. Broken pieces of petrified flesh clattered over the floor, and whatever had brought the crocodile back to life after many thousands of years slipped away in drifting strips of black linen and clouds of grey dust.

5

The python shook his head and lifted from the floor with a hiss of anger. Had he seen the Major lift his club to kill him? Ramses did not stay to find out.

After he caught up to Felicity and Sharrif, they dashed into a passageway and nearly collided with a second crocodile mummy. It lay in the center of the passageway floor, facing them with a rustling hiss and sightless eyes. "Wrong way," Ramses said, and they backed away and ran past a second ram sphinx into a different passageway. They met several more mummies as they ran, and each time they veered off into a new direction. It seemed, to Ramses, they were being guided by the mummies, and forced onto certain paths – but paths to where? And to what? He could not guess.

They came to another mummy. Another hiss. Another direction. This time, Ramses saluted with his paw and said, "Thanks mate," before darting off into the gloom. "Follow the name of the king," he called out as they fled. "Follow the rams, always the rams. And pay attention to where the crocodile mummies tell us to go. Stay together!"

Heavy footsteps sounded behind them, running. *Clomp! Clomp! Clomp!*

Sharrif started to hide the lantern in the folds of his robe but saw no point. Pickelhaube knew where they were. Seconds later, he stopped beneath a towering statue of Amenemhat III. "Oh no." Sharrif held out the lantern. Its flame began to sputter. "It's running out of oil."

This had not entered any of their minds. Even Ramses hadn't thought of it. He could see in even the dimmest starlight, but down here? With solid stone blocking all light of every kind?

"The candle is back with that first crocodile," Ramses said. "We'll never find it again."

"I have matches," Sharrif said. "If the lantern dies, we can use those. Until we run out."

The flame sputtered again. Its feeble glow showed them another sphinx, many times larger than those before. Its massive lion's body bore a ram's head with curled horns.

"How is it possible no one knows it's here?" Felicity asked, astounded.

"Your uncle still doesn't know," Ramses said. "He has no idea all this lies beneath our campsite. How I wish he were with us. Nothing he likes more than a bit of a pickle."

The note of sadness in Ramses' voice alarmed Felicity. She would rather lose the last of the lantern's flame than the last of

Ramses' optimism. If he gave up, what hope did they have? "We'll find a way," she whispered. "Don't you think?"

He shook his fur. "I do," he said after a second's pause. "Yes, yes, I certainly do! We have not come to the end yet. Something will turn up."

They approached a gateway nearly as large as the Sobek Gate. This time they passed through without a hint of thunder. The light slap of their feet upon the stone came back to them in hollow echoes.

Sharrif held up the frail light. Useless. They saw only darkness, endless darkness.

A sudden trace of fragrance met their nostrils, a sweet smell of incense smoke. How could that be?

"Stop," Ramses whispered. His voice quivered and echoed like Sharrif's voice in the Nilometer so long ago. "*Stop-stop-op-op-op...*"

Heavy footsteps clomped behind them, approaching the gate. Lantern light appeared on the base of the colossal ram sphinx.

Ramses waved his paw at Sharrif to tell him to turn off the last flicker of lantern flame. The moment he did, a new light appeared, sudden and unexpected. Torches burst into flame, one by one, along all four walls of a massive chamber. They filled it with firelight so bright that Felicity and Sharrif had to shield their eyes. Ramses' eyes adjusted immediately, and he took in a scene that nailed him in place with wonder.

A host of blackened crocodile mummies lined the walls, all facing inward. Another crocodile mummy lay in the center of the chamber, separated from the others and wrapped from snout to tail in crisp snow-white linens.

Behind the newly wrapped mummy, a stone platform rose a foot above the floor. Upon this stood an altar made of solid gold, nearly hidden within a hoard of gold and silver objects and chests of gemstones. Clouds of incense rose from golden censers on each side of the altar.

Felicity lowered her hands and gazed at the scene, astounded. "Where *are* we?"

"A lost temple to Sobek," Ramses returned, and he studied the mummies along the walls.

"But the incense," Sharrif said. "And those torches...who lit them?"

The incense clouds drifted over the golden altar and began to thicken.

Sounds passed over them, coming from...where? The altar? The smoke? It was an ancient sound, a chanting sound, a sound not heard on this earth for many hundreds of years and filled with words no one then alive could understand.

The smoke spiraled in place and, to their eyes, began to gather into human form. Bare arms...bare legs...smoky white loin-cloths...though they could not make out a face of any kind.

"Who are they?" Sharrif asked.

Before anyone could answer, Pickelhaube appeared behind them. He strode into the chamber, holding up his lantern and squinting as if trying to see in the darkness. Umbalali slithered beside him, looking from side to side as if he, too, could not see the torches, the incense figures, and the gold.

Felicity and Sharrif tensed to run but Ramses stopped them with a whispered, "Stay. They're blind to all this."

He moved silently away from them and sat in his accustomed position with his tail wrapped around his paws. "Pickelpuss." *icklep-uss-puss-puss.*

The giant froze. He cocked his head, listening. He set the lantern on the floor and pulled his club from his belt.

"Here, kitty, kitty, kitty," Umbalali hissed. The bloody claw marks on his face oozed.

Ramses padded to the other side of Felicity and Sharrif without making a sound. He smirked and said, "Here snakey, snakey,

snakey," *akey-akey-akey*. Pickelhaube and the python turned his way, squinting.

He did it again, moving silently to another spot. "Here Pickel-tickle-snickle-puss," *uss-uss-uss*. The two scoundrels spun about, following his voice.

Felicity tapped Sharrif and pointed toward the side of the altar. She hoped they could get around to the back without Pickelhaube hearing them, but when she took a step, her toe struck a golden object on the floor and sent it clanging.

Pickelhaube did not hesitate. He now knew their general direction and he began to swing his club. The lethal metal tip hummed through the air.

"Run!" Felicity said. Sharrif turned to follow, but Pickelhaube sprang toward him faster than expected. He caught Sharrif by the sleeve and dragged him to his knees. He lifted his club.

Ramses dashed toward him, prepared to leap, but an unexpected roar as loud as the thunder at the Sobek Gate stopped him in his tracks.

It stopped Pickelhaube too, with his arm in the air and club poised to come down.

"Behind you!" Umbalali cried, looking from side to side in wide-eyed panic. "Beside you! All *around* you!"

Pickelhaube turned to him, confused. The python did not linger. He squealed with terror and spun about and slithered from the cavern through the gate.

Pickelhaube turned and turned, staring into what (for him) was only darkness but for Ramses and Felicity was all too horribly clear. "Run Sharrif!" she cried, and he rolled away from Pickelhaube and leaped to his feet.

Crocodile mummies lurched from their places along the walls. They rumbled and hissed toward the giant from all directions. Rotten linens snapped as jaws crackled open. Black teeth glistened. Sightless eyes focused unseeing upon their prey.

They moved in and Pickelhaube finally saw his peril. He brought his club down upon the first. *Thunk!* The mummy collapsed in a cloud of dust. A second came from behind, and again – *crunch!* Powdery dust lifted around him. A third caught him on the boot. He reached down to push it away and a fourth snapped its ancient jaws around his arm.

Major Pickelhaube slammed his club down over and over but there were too many and they came too fast.

Down came his club – this time, a mummy snatched it from his hand.

They dragged him to his knees, the same way he had dragged Sharrif to his knees only moments before. Pickelhaube punched. He slapped. He clawed at them, but he could not hold them back. He could not scream. He could not cry out. After a final desperate effort to rise, they pulled him down again and he fell in silence.

The crocodiles swarmed over him with a dusty roar, and they swarmed until nothing remained of Major Hermann-Düüfus von Pickelhaube but a club broken into splinters, a dented helmet, and a single bloody sleeve.

The crocodiles growled and hissed and milled about in search of more prey.

"What'll we do?" Felicity asked. She picked up the golden object that first alerted Pickelhaube. It was a *uraeus* crown with a golden cobra attached to the front, rearing up in striking position. She held it close, as if it might protect her from the swarming crocodiles.

It didn't work.

They moved toward them – not with the same fury and roar of the attack on Pickelhaube, but on they came, steady, plodding, coming in from all sides.

The incense figures did the same from the altar.

Within seconds, Felicity and Sharrif stood back to back with Ramses at their feet.

"Their blue crocodile," Ramses whispered. "Offer it to them."

Felicity slipped her arm through the golden *uraeus* and pulled the broken pieces of the blue crocodile from her pocket. Ramses led her toward the altar. "The Sacred Crocodile," he called to the smoky figures. She held the pieces out at arms-length, clattering in her shaking hands.

"The *Petsuchos*," Ramses called. "The Son of Sobek returned to you now."

The incense figures drifted closer. A smoky hand appeared before Felicity, reaching. It touched the broken crocodile. The pieces quivered. Flecks of blue glaze crackled. Felicity gasped in dismay when the pieces crumbled into dust that ran through her fingers.

Ramses stared at it, bewildered.

The incense figures drifted past him, and from behind, he heard a soft, small voice. "Pet," Timsah said within the folds of Sharrif's robe. Sharrif could not turn away from the scene before him. "Not a pet, you're a friend," he said in a distracted way.

"Pet," Timsah said again, and again Sharrif told him no, he was not a pet, he was a friend, and "*Pet*," the crocodile said again.

This time Sharrif froze. He stared straight ahead. "Pet," he whispered.

He sank to his knees and opened a fold of his robe.

Timsah sat upon his lap, gazing up at him with wise and knowing eyes, ancient and gentle and as old as the Nile, and Sharrif's own eyes widened in shock. "*Pet-suchos!*" he whispered.

Felicity heard him. "It's gone," she said, staring down at the dust.

"That wasn't it," Sharrif said without taking his eyes off his little friend. "That was *never* it."

Ramses looked at him, looked at the crocodile on his lap, and everything clicked into place at once.

The newly-wrapped mummy. Its time had come and gone, the same as it had for every one of the ancient crocodiles in the necropolis.

All had been the sacred crocodile at one time. All had been the *Petsuchos*. All had been the pampered and worshiped Son of Sobek, and all had passed away after a long and happy life...and all had been replaced.

They *had* to be replaced. It was the only way to keep the god of the Nile at peace.

This was why the crocodile mummies had come to their aid time and time again. Not to save Uncle Alistair, or Sharrif, or Felicity, or Ramses.

They did it for Timsah.

The mummies were at the Temple of Kom Ombo where they found him.

Timsah was fishing with Ramses when the mummies floated by.

Timsah was in the water with Uncle Alistair and Ramses when the mummies tossed him from the river onto the boat.

He was with Sharrif on the sandbar when the mummies chased off the pirates.

They had done it all for Timsah.

They had watched over him.

They had protected him.

They had guided them into the center of the Labyrinth for Timsah was the newly appointed sacred crocodile. Timsah was the Son of Sobek. Timsah was the *Petsuchos,* and his time had come at last.

6

Smoke thickened around them. The chanting grew louder and deeper. The misty hands reached for Timsah, the living sacred crocodile. Sharrif tried to push them away, but his own hands passed harmlessly through the mist and on they came.

They lifted Timsah. Sharrif saw it clearly but for Felicity and Ramses standing only feet away, it appeared the baby crocodile rose from Sharrif's lap on his own.

His tail dangled. His feet hung down.

Sharrif reached for him, but the smoky hands took on stronger form and gently pushed him back. "Timsah!" he called and his voice cracked.

Ramses strode up to Sharrif. "Let him go."

Sharrif's breath caught in his chest as he fought back his tears. "You think he'll be dangerous when he gets bigger, but I know him. He wouldn't hurt me, he would never hurt me."

Ramses set a paw on Sharrif's foot. "Not in a million years." Tears sprang to the boy's eyes. He scooped the cat up into his arms and held him close and Ramses rubbed his cheek against his face. "Not in a *hundred* million years," Ramses purred.

Felicity set her hand upon Sharrif's arm. "Not in a hundred thousand million years," she whispered.

Her hand suddenly tightened. "What's that?" She pointed to a trickle of water at the base of the golden altar.

It rolled through the mounded treasure before dropping over the edge of the platform to the stone floor. More water appeared at the walls of the chamber, gushing in without a sound. In less than a minute, a half inch of water had covered the entire floor of the cavern.

Ramses hopped down from Sharrif's arms. He sniffed the water and lifted his paws, one at a time, shaking them. "Oh no…"

He nodded toward the crocodile in the white linen. "When the last Son of Sobek died, the Nile went with him."

"The drought," Felicity said.

Ramses nodded. "But now..."

Her eyes widened. "But now there's a new Son, and now the floods return."

The water rose another half inch. Something cracked in the distance. A low wave gurgled through the main door and swirled around their feet, now three inches. "How deep will it get?" Sharrif asked.

"Too deep for me," Ramses said, and he hopped back onto his shoulder.

Felicity studied the flood damage on the walls, rising to a height of four feet in some places, six in others. "If it rises that high..."

chirp chirp chirp!

Timsah squirmed from the smoky hands and dropped down before the altar into the water. The smoky figures followed.

Sharrif ran splashing to him with Ramses on his shoulder. "Come with us!" he cried and lifted Timsah into his arms.

croak croak

Sharrif waded backward to avoid the grasping smoke.

"You don't have to stay," he said to his friend. "You don't have to be the *Petsuchos!*"

chirp chirp I do I am chirp

Ramses tapped Timsah with his paw. "Do you know a way out, little leathery friend?"

The crocodile twisted in Sharrif's arms and looked into the boy's eyes. "*Chomp.*"

Sharrif returned the crocodile's gaze, confused. Why would he bring up his game with the sticks? Why *now?*

"*Chomp,*" Timsah said again, firmly, and Sharrif stroked the top of his head. "We can't play now," he said with a sad smile.

"It isn't stopping," Felicity said, alarmed. Another crack in the distance sent in a new gush of water. "Come Sharrif!"

"*Chomp,*" Timsah said. "*chirp chirp go — chomp, chomp, Chomp!*" Sharrif straightened, his face suddenly pale.

"What is he saying?" Felicity asked, frustrated by the delay.

"He's telling me to play."

"*Now?*" she asked, astounded.

"Yes, now. But not with the sticks. The game! He's telling me to follow pattern of the game, his path through the sticks. We played it so much, I memorized it. He made sure I did. He must have known this would happen."

chrip chirp chirp Timsah squealed, and Sharrif hugged him close. "*Bye friend bite chomp love bye friend bye,*" the little crocodile said, and "bye friend love bye," Sharrif whispered in return.

He set him down in the water. The little crocodile swam away and scrambled onto the platform and once again he rose in the embrace of the smoky hands. "Chomp!" he called to Sharrif as he drifted toward the golden altar. "Chomp!"

The water rose to their knees. Felicity waded to the nearest wall and pulled two torches from their sconces. She handed one to Sharrif. Ramses leaped from the boy's shoulder to hers: "Let's go."

Sharrif backed away, holding his torch. His eyes filled with tears. He had so many things he wanted to say, but he could not say them, even if he tried.

Felicity called to him and ran from the cavern with Ramses on her shoulder. Sharrif followed but stopped at the doorway for a final look. What he saw next, he would never be able to fully describe.

Timsah lay upon the golden altar on a stretch of new linen. Smoky priests hovered around him, bedecking him with jewels and precious ornaments.

Another figure emerged from the smoke behind the altar, much larger than all the others. Higher it rose, twenty feet high, then thirty, lifting into the torchlight with eyes black and sparkling, a powerful figure with the muscular chest of a man and the head of a ferocious crocodile. "Old Crocodile Head," Sharrif realized with a gasp. "Sobek!"

And in the towering figure, on the towering figure, and somehow *through* him, Sharrif saw the light of the sun shining upon a world of green reeds and crystal-clear water filled with silvery fish, and in this vision, he also saw the thundering clouds sweeping over distant highlands and showering the hills and the rising river with their life-giving rains.

This all happened in a matter of seconds, but it was enough. Sharrif would never after imagine Timsah alone in a cold and barren world of the dead. His friend would live in that sunny, watery world of his vision, and he would live out a long and happy life as the adored and pampered *Petsuchos*, the luckiest crocodile along the entire length of the Nile.

7

Old Crocodile Head's appearance brought on a sudden clash of thunderclouds in the Ethiopian highlands, thousands of miles away. Rain fell and fell, and more clouds formed, and more rain fell. The water would soon find the river and the river would soon rise. The Nilometer at Kom Ombo would fill to a height unseen in many years. The dry lands would drink deep and the riverbanks would blossom into green.

But then, at that moment, only the Faiyum saw the rising floods, and only in the depths of the Labyrinth of the Crocodiles.

When Sharrif passed through the gate, he held up his torch and read the water swirling around the base of the colossal ram.

Whirlpools swept by, leading off to the right.

"Not that way!" he called to Felicity. "It's flowing in this direction."

She spun around and rejoined him in front of the sphinx, still holding the cobra *uraeus*. The churning water bewildered her. "Now what?"

"Chomp!" Sharrif called. "It's the only way out." He looked down. "This is the water." He looked up again and pointed at one of the plain unpainted stone columns. "And *those* are the sticks!"

Deep rumblings sounded deep within the Labyrinth.

Water rose. Water hissed. Water rushed and splashed and slapped against the statues.

"This way," Sharrif shouted, and he led them toward another plain limestone column. "And there," he cried, making a sharp turn toward another.

Water swirled up to Felicity's waist. White foam bubbled on the surface. Crocodile mummies floated past, now completely lifeless and banging into each other like floating logs.

"You're sure?" Ramses called.

"I am," Sharrif said. "After that column, we need to make an S curve around two more and then a sharp right and two swings to the left."

"Right-o," Ramses said, impressed. "Carry on."

The water churned higher.

"Don't stop!" Sharrif called over the sloshing waves. "Keep moving!"

"I'm trying!" Felicity held the torch in one hand and the *uraeus* in the other, her arms up high. "This current is too strong."

"Push through it!" Sharrif shouted. "This way! This way!"

A new rush of water struck Felicity from the side. It washed over her and snatched Ramses from her shoulder. Her torch shot from her hand and disappeared with a hiss.

"Ramses!" she cried when she popped to the surface. She flailed about, searching through the black water. "Ramses! Where are you?!"

"This way, Felicity!" Sharrif called in the distance. He waved his torch over his head.

"I can't find Ramses!"

A splash and splutter came from behind. "Here!" the cat cried. He clung to the edge of a doorway, with his front claws clutching the stone, barely holding on.

Felicity slipped her wrist through the *uraeus* and pushed it up over her shoulder. Using her arms, she fought the current. "Hold on!"

A wave crested over Ramses. His claws slipped. He lost his grip. The water swept him into a dizzying churn.

He shot past Felicity. She caught one of his forelegs. She lifted him, fearing she would break it, but she had no choice.

Ramses rose coughing.

He clutched her wrist with all four paws and she pulled him close. He climbed onto her shoulder, still coughing. "Don't lose Sharrif!"

The current had pushed the boy further away, nearly out of view. "This way!" he called. "This way!"

"Hold on tight," Felicity said. She felt Ramses tighten his paws upon her shoulder. She leaned forward. Her feet left the floor and she rode the waves, dashing through the columns on a path toward Sharrif. He waited for her with one hand around a pillar and struggling to keep the torch burning with the other.

Felicity shot past him, unable to stop.

Sharrif released the pillar. Water sloshed over him and extinguished his torch, and now they raced through the halls in utter darkness, as helpless as driftwood surging down a swollen river.

They could not see. They could not call.

Felicity felt a sudden dip, as if the current had taken her over a low waterfall. Her ears popped from a change in pressure and *whoosh*! Out she flew in a rush of hissing foam, out through a crack in the rocks, out into the clear night air and into the canal beside the Pyramid of Hawara.

Sharrif was already there, coughing and climbing through the shallows toward the shore, and – "Felicity!" she heard. "Take my hand!"

"Uncle Alistair!"

He strode through the churning canal, reaching for her. The golden cobra *uraeus* had slipped down her arm and she held it out, clutched in her fist. Uncle Alistair grabbed the other side. "Hold on tight!" With the *ureaus* firmly in his grip, he towed her to shore and to Sharrif waiting upon the sand.

'Ramses," she cried. "Where's Ramses?"

"Still here," he said at her ear, clinging to her shoulder. "A bit moist, but here."

"Oh, Uncle!" she cried when he lifted her into an embrace. "I thought I'd never see you again."

"But you have, my dear, you have. Come now, all of you. Come sit by the fire. I'll put the kettle on for tea and you'll be dry in no time. You too, old boy," he said to Ramses. "What a sight you are. Sopping wet from whiskers to tail. I suspect an adventure of some kind."

8

The river pirates guarding the Countess and Uncle Alistair panicked when the ground quaked beneath what they still believed was the solid bedrock floor of the Labyrinth. When the unexpected gush of water thundered from the earthen bank of the canal, they slithered and ran from the camp in wild-eyed terror.

"We've seen the last of them, I trust," Uncle Alistair said as he built up the campfire to brew a strong pot of tea. "All very mysterious, if you ask me."

"Which no one did," the Countess muttered but Uncle Alistair ignored her. "So tell me," he said, turning to his soaking-wet friends. "The last I saw, you were dashing into the desert with that giant gargoyle and python close behind."

Felicity and Sharrif told only the most unimportant details. The Countess lay opposite the fire, coiled in front of her basket. They knew enough not to mention the treasure of the crocodiles in front of the greedy cobra. They did not talk about Timsah either. They did not even mention the presence of the monumental Labyrinth lying below their feet. Such details could wait until they were back in Cairo and out of sight of the Countess.

They did tell her of Pickelhaube's end, but said he had fallen into an unseen shaft inside the pyramid. Whether or not she believed them, they did not know as she only sniffed and said, "Good riddanthe."

Uncle Alistair poked at the fire with a stick to brighten the flames. As the firelight flared, the cobra's eyes suddenly opened so wide her monocle fell to the sand. "And what have we here?"

Felicity tried to hide the *uraeus* in the folds of Sharrif's robe, but the Countess had already spotted a glint of gold. "May I thee it, young man?" she asked, and she batted her eyes at him.

Sharrif did not move.

He did not say a word.

"I owe you a thinthere apology, my dear boy," the Countess said with no sincerity at all. "Thorry." She sniffed and sighed as if relieved to get *that* over with. "Now then. The gold…may I thee it?"

Sharrif held up the *ureaus*. "And that is as close as you'll get, you perfectly ridiculous serpent."

The cobra's half-smile disappeared into a scowl.

Sharrif shrugged, unconcerned.

They all looked up when they heard a sudden eerie trilling call from the desert.

"So Umbalali lives still," Ramses said and, like Sharrif a moment before, he shrugged, unconcerned.

Before anyone could say anything further, and before Sharrif could once again fold the *ureaus* into his robe, the Countess suddenly reared up. Her eyes glittered with greed and her fury erupted like a venomous volcano. "That'th mine, you rotten little thneak!"

Her mouth sprang open to reveal her single fang and she shot across the sand toward Sharrif.

He fell back with a gasp, his hand rose up, and the cobra's fang connected with the golden crown – *clang!*

Her fang cracked and off it went, flying through the air. The Countess shrieked, horrified, and she stared wildly around, like an ancient toothless hag searching for her lost dentures.

"My fang!" she cried. "My last beloved glorious fang! This is your fault!" she yelled at Sharrif. "What have you done with it, you horrid little beast?"

Sharrif quickly recovered. He dropped the *ureaus* into the reed sarcophagus and closed the lid with a click.

"You think that will stop me, you simpleton?" the cobra cried, glaring at him. "I may not have fangs to poison you, but I can strangle you all the same, you...you...you..." Her toothless mouth dropped open and she stared into space with a shocked expression.

"Ssssstrangle you all the ssssame," she repeated, emphasizing the S sounds. She paused again, still staring into space, and then came a single delicate drawn-out, "ssssssssssssssssssss."

She looked at the others and her toothless face twisted into the most gruesome smile imaginable. "I can hiss," she said. "Lisssssten! Sssssssssssssssssssss! I can *hiss* again!"

"And you may take it with you," said Uncle Alistair. When she cast her greedy eye at the sarcophagus, he added, "Not the gold, you unpleasant wretch. You'll never get that. I meant your newfound hiss. You may take it back to the Rose and Venom or out into the desert or wherever you jolly well choose to go, as long as it is far from us."

"You haven't sssssseen the lasssst of me," the Countess hissed with a sneer. "Look for me when you leassst expect it. And there I shall be, a sssnake in the grassssss!"

"To do what, gum us to death?" Uncle Alistair asked, and she snarled and turned from the fire.

"Be on your guard, ssssimpleton," she hissed at Sharrif as she left, and they heard her long after she slithered into the darkness, grumbling, and trying out her new hiss with as many S-words as possible. "Asssstrounding assortment of dissssssrespectful ssssssspecimensss of nasssstinessssss, every lasssssssst one of you perfectly ridiculoussss ssssssscoundrelsssss, if you asssk me."

Uncle Alistair cupped his hands to the sides of his mouth and called out: "Which no one did."

....and that was that. Her hisses faded into the desert and only the crackling flames of the campfire remained.

"Good riddanthe," said Ramses with a smirk, and the others laughed.

"Let her stew in her own misery for a time," said Uncle Alistair, gazing out into the desert. "She'll get over it soon enough and show up again to cause a spot of trouble. Her kind always does."

Felicity, Ramses, and Sharrif spent a good hour or so filling in Uncle Alistair on all that happened and all they had seen. He listened, fascinated, adding only an occasional, "Oh, I say," and "jolly interesting," and "How I wish I'd been with you in that particular pickle."

Ramses finished by saying, "And now it's all gone, once again hidden under the flood waters of the Labyrinth. Ah, well."

"No matter," said Uncle Alistair, and he meant it. "We shall undoubtedly have more adventures and new tales to tell."

"And more pickles to find our way out of," Felicity added.

"That too," her uncle said. "Always that."

Ramses looked out at the desert. "I admire her in a way..."

"Admire who? Admire the Countess?" said Uncle Alistair. "Oh, surely not, Ramses."

"I do!" the cat insisted. "Old Perfectly Ridiculous is a talented thief and cheat. No one better." He pawed at the sarcophagus holding the golden crown. "I certainly do not admire *what* she does, but how she does it? Masterful."

"Stuff and nonsense," said Uncle Alistair.

Ramses sat back on his haunches and threw his front paws into the air. "Find your passion, Jammpot!" he said with a laugh. "Find the thing that makes you happy and give it your all, the way she does."

"Lying, cheating, stealing, living life as a nasty, wholly unlikeable character – these are her passions?"

"Of course they are," Ramses said. "She takes no trouble to hide who she is and what she does. Why should she? It makes no sense to be someone you cannot be, or more important, someone you do not *want* to be." He turned to Sharrif and lowered his paws. "Am I right?"

Sharrif smiled. "You are, Ramses Faro. You are."

"Then let's get some sleep, shall we? We'll start off first thing in the morning, back to the *Wind Cat*. We owe people money for books and boats. We'll haul the anchor, raise the sails, and you, Sharrif Aziz, Master Sailor, can set us on our course." The boy glanced over his shoulder at the Pyramid of Hawara but said nothing. "You'll see him again," Ramses said, reading his mind. "Old friends have ways of turning up in unexpected places at unexpected times."

Felicity sat down beside Sharrif. "They have ways of surprising us too. They turn out to be much stronger and much more clever than we ever imagined."

"That they do," Ramses said. "Come Jammpot," he called. "Felicity. You too, Sharrif. Curl up by the fire for a long and lovely catnap."

As the others stood and began to prepare their camp for the night, Uncle Alistair asked, "And what of you? I suppose you will be standing watch, as usual."

Ramses gazed up at the pyramid of Hawara and the stars beyond, blazing and twinkling in a silent sky and he wrapped his tail around his paws, and he smiled at his particular friend and said, "And I suppose you may be right, old boy."

Ramses Faro

GLOSSARY

Amenemhat III: Egyptian pharaoh, 12th Dynasty of the Middle Kingdom, from 1860 to 1814 BC. He oversaw the construction of the Egyptian Labyrinth and the nearby Hawara Pyramid, which also served as his royal tomb.

Amun: a powerful god, often considered the creator god or supreme deity.

Asp: another name for the Egyptian cobra, most famously used by Cleopatra to commit suicide.

Basbousa: a traditional Egyptian cake sweetened with honey, rose water or orange blossom water.

Cartouche: a carving or painting of an oval surrounding a group of hieroglyphs, most often depicting the name of a pharaoh.

Dahabeeya: A traditional passenger vessel of the Nile, often luxurious. It is a barge-like vessel with two sails and an upper deck covered with an awning.

Dynasty: A powerful group or family who ruled Egypt for long periods of time, sometimes over many generations. There were 32 dynasties in ancient Egypt, grouped into Old, Middle, or New Kingdoms (or into Intermediate Periods separating each of these Kingdoms).

Faience: A ceramic glaze widely used for beads, scarabs, amulets and small statues. Often in a color known as Egyptian Blue, the method for making this color is no longer known.

Faiyum Oasis: a depression in the desert connected by a canal to the Nile, about 70 miles southwest of Cairo.

Felucca: traditional wooden sailboat used along the Nile, using oars and a single mast with one triangular sail (called a lateen sail)

Hawara: An archeological site near Crocodilopolis (The City of Crocodiles) at the entrance to the Faiyum Oasis. (See also **Pyramid of Hawara** below)

Herodotus: An ancient Greek writer, sometimes called "The Father of History" as he is the first known author to focus on historical subjects. Lived from approximately 484 BC to 425 BC.

Hieroglyphic: a system of writing used by the ancient Egyptians, using symbols and drawings instead of letters. The symbols are **Hieroglyphs**. The adjective **Hieroglyphic** is used to describe the form of writing.

Karnak: A vast temple built near the city of Luxor, built over the course of two millennia (approximately 2055 BC – 100 AD). It is one of the largest religious complexes in the world.

Kom Ombo: a unique double temple in upper Egypt, with one half dedicated to the falcon god Horus and other to the crocodile god Sobek. Kom Ombo is most famous now for its collection of mummified crocodiles discovered at the site.

Labyrinth: an elaborate maze, sometimes created inside a structure such as the Greek Labyrinth built by Daedalus to house the fearsome Minotaur and the Egyptian Labyrinth built in the Faiyum Oasis by Pharaoh Amenemhat III.

Necropolis: an ancient Greek word meaning "city of the dead" – a large cemetery or burial site.

Nilometer: a structure used to measure the level of water during the traditional Nile floods. There are three varieties: a vertical column, a stairway leading down to the river, or a deep well.

Sir William Flinders Petrie: (June 3, 1853 – July 28, 1942) A British Egyptologist, rediscovered the entrance to the Pyramid of Hawara and the looted burial chamber of pharaoh Amenemhat III in 1888.

Petsuchos: a living Nile crocodile considered the "son of Sobek" and worshipped with gold and precious gems by the temple priests.

Pharaoh: the name of the Egyptian king, beginning with Menes in 3200 BC and ending with Cleopatra's death on August 12, 30 BC.

Pyramid of Hawara: Built in the Faiyum Oasis during the 12th Dynasty as a burial tomb and monument for Amenemhat III. It was made of mud bricks encased in limestone. Much of it has been damaged by a canal built in later centuries.

Sarcophagus: A coffin, or container to hold a coffin, most often made of stone, but sometimes made of wood.

Sobek: the god of the Nile, shown as a man with a crocodile head. Live sacred crocodiles were kept at his temples in Kom Ombo and in the Faiyum Oasis. After death, these crocodiles were mummified in his honor.

Sphinx: a mythical creature with the head of a human, a falcon, a cat or a sheep and the body of a lion. Considered a guardian, their statues are often found at the entrance to a temple or royal tomb.

Uraeus: a symbol of the authority of the pharaoh, shown as an upright cobra. Can be used on a headband, a hieroglyphic, a statue or as part of a royal crown (as seen on the royal mask of Tutankhamun)

Acknowledgements

Much of *Ramses Faro and the Labyrinth of the Crocodiles* was written in the north of Peru, where the author was trapped during the pandemic of 2020. Many helped him then, and since, with comments and criticism, starting with his intrepid band of readers: first, his first readers Jens Kohler and his sons Oscar and Simon, followed by a cavalcade of insightful and helpful critics: Lilly Cataldi-Simmers, Stephanie Cunningham, Larry Graykin and the 6th grade members of the Time and Space Exploring Detective Association (TaSEDA) at the Barrington, NH Middle School; Thomas Gross, Michael Walsh, and, most especially, Jude Bascom.

He also thanks Susan Perlman Cohen for her patience, her guidance and ever-helpful suggestions, Kevin O'Connor for his early support and advice, Spiros Simeonidis (and Lancelot) for their friendship and Greek translations, Anne Ford, Vitali Aukhimovich and Kerry O'Malley for their cheerleading and encouragement.

For matters related to felines, he thanks Kim Sprecher, Sarah Mucho, Holly Melton Ward, and especially Frankie Jalbert and Amanda Sprecher; Mandarin and Cashel for knocking papers onto the floor and hiding pens when required; and to Ramses himself, whose antics served as the inspiration for this, the first in a series of Ramses Faro adventures.

Coming soon!

Ramses Faro
and
The Lost Army of Persia

In the year 525 B.C. an army of 50,000 Persian soldiers disappeared in the Western Desert of Egypt, overwhelmed and buried alive by a monstrous sandstorm.

Over 2,000 years later, Ramses Faro and his friends are in Port Said to see Felicity off on a steamship bound for London and her strict Aunt Ludmilla-Florence. They meet a stranger on the dock who begs Uncle Alistair to act as courier and bring a mysterious package to Dr. Roxanne Heydari at the British Museum. After the stranger meets an untimely and violent end, they discover his package contains a marvelous golden sword of great age and priceless value.

When Dr. Heydari, a glamorous silver-furred Perian cat, arrives in Egypt, she joins Ramses and Company as they follow the clues connected with golden sword in the hope of discovering the long-lost Army of the Persians.

But will the treacherous Sir Boneyface Graveyard and his band of assassins stop them? Find out in this new Ramses Faro adventure, as they embark on their wild dash from Port Said to Cairo and out into the deadly sands of the Sahara.

Ramses Faro

Other Books by
John-Richard Thompson

The Christmas Mink
The Battle-Ravens

(with Anne Ford)
Laughing Allegra
On Their Own
A Special Mother
The Forgotten Child
The Stigmatized Child
A Fascinating Life

For more, visit: www.j-rt.com

Printed in Great Britain
by Amazon